I0748676

Bat Crap Crazy

Bat Crap Crazy

CJ Hanlon

Joyce Mathers Grant LLC

Cover and Text Design by: CJ Hanlon

A CIP record for this book is acailable from the Library of Congress Cataloging-in-Publication Data

ISBN-13: 979-8-9905269-0-7 (Paperback Edition)
ISBN-13: 979-8-9905269-1-4 (eBook Edition)
Published by:

Joyce Mathers Grant LLC
529 E. 11th Ave

Denver, CO 80206

To the underdogs.

Author's Note:

Bat Crap Crazy (BCC) was conceived in November 2013 as part of a challenge to write a 50,000-word novel in a month.[1] By Thanksgiving, I had written 50,000 words, but the book was far from complete. Over the next seven years, the loosely formed story about a virus sat in a virtual desk drawer while real life happened. Then, in 2020, COVID shut the world down, and I had the opportunity to focus on writing again.

I wanted to return to BCC and fill out the missing pieces of the story, but I wondered if I had unknowingly written a story that too closely mirrored what was unfolding before us. Nevertheless, I quietly began to expand the plot because I still loved it. The story's writing was cathartic because it helped me explore my feelings and emotions about what was happening in the news and in my neighborhood in the early days of the pandemic. It also gave me the perspective needed for a situation no one could control.

In November of 2021, I found an online community of writers called Shut Up & Write.[2] I signed in every morning and wrote or rewrote for an hour and a half. Before too long, the second and third drafts of the book were complete. In the process, I added, deleted, rearranged, and changed large chunks of the book.

The most significant change I made was a monumental shift

1 Visit https://nanowrimo.org/ for more information.

2 Visit https://www.shutupwrite.com/ for more information.

in the primary point of view from Bailey Dayton to Anita Belo. I quite simply think Anita has a more compelling, albeit horrid, story to tell. Bailey's character is too mainstream to explore the lengths to which a person would go to save their own life.

Even before Anita contracts the Marburg Virus[3], she is a self-absorbed individual, but once she is faced with her own mortality, she no longer cares what it costs to survive. She has one goal and one goal only and does mind-boggling things to save her own life. The rest is collateral damage. Her story is as linear as it gets. As the novel unfolds and more characters get sucked into her quest, you realize that life isn't at all linear; it is a spider web of complex systems.

We live under the false belief that we are rugged individuals capable of surviving anything on our own when, in fact, our society's framework is complicated and fragile.

The pandemic proved that a dystopian wasteland isn't as much a fantasy movie as we once believed. In truth, we have much more in common with each other in our shared experience of the world, be it good, bad, or indifferent. We need each other, and we often don't know what personal struggles another person is going through, But what BCC makes clear is how those struggles may affect your own life.

One final thought: Anita will disgust and anger you. Her actions will challenge you to keep reading, but remember, she has an essential message about facing the fear of death. Bat Crap Crazy isn't a love story or a cozy mystery. It is a tale with an important lesson that taught me to get comfortable with being uncomfortable. I ask you to do the same.

---

3 Visit https://www.who.int/news-room/fact-sheets/detail/marburg-virus-disease for more information.

Part I

Prologue:

August 1967 - Neu Leben Laboratories, Marburg, West Germany

Monkey 842 slumped in the back corner of her cage and whimpered while the research team stood around her last friend on an exam table. She raised her furry hands to cover her ears and shield her from the constant beeps of the machines. A loud, painful moan escaped her lips as the beeps slowed and turned into a steady, high-pitched note. She cried because she knew she was alone now.

Monkey 842 paced in her cage. The pen rocked on the shelf when her pace quickened. As she moved, she harmonized an out-of-control scream with the heart monitor. The fourth time she hit the side of the cage, it tipped and crashed to the lab floor.

The crash scared the humans. Four of the eight humans looked at what caused it. Then, before anyone could figure it out, Monkey 842 was out of her cage. She danced around the room, her arms flailing, her eyes wide. Instead of attempting to restrain the wild animal, in the panic, the humans made a path as she charged to the exam table.

She yanked the cords and released them from the heart monitor. The room fell silent, and the humans watched as Monkey 842 mounted the table and cradled her dead friend's body. She swayed with her eyes closed and whimpered.

One human reached for a tranquilizer gun and shot her with phencyclidine in the back of the neck. Monkey 842 opened her eyes wide, released the body, and swung her furry arms violently. She caught the tech off guard, and he stumbled backward. Then, before he could recover, she reared up on her hind legs and jumped off the table onto a researcher. The drug slowed her down, but she still pinned the man to the floor. She looked him square in the eyes before she bit his neck. Blood spurted everywhere from the severed carotid artery.

1: Anita

August 1966 – Collo, Angola Africa

Anita rushed home after school, excited to share the perfect grade she got on her science test. As she approached the front door of her home, she heard her mother's voice. It wasn't the calm and patient tone most typical of her mother. She crept up to the door and waited. She huddled under the window to listen to the conversation, surprised to hear her father's voice.

"Sara, this matter is not negotiable. Therefore, I am taking this opportunity. It will benefit the entire family."

"Dominique, I left Portugal and followed you to Angola because you said we could have a better life. And we did, but now we are in the middle of a war. So, maybe you should work on getting us out of Angola as a family instead of leaving us behind."

"The Angolan War of Independence is not our war. Don't forget, we are Portuguese. Therefore, I can leave anytime I want."

Sara snapped back. "What about the rest of us?"

"You are my wife. You will do what I say," Dominique snapped back. "I'll go to Uganda and make the money we need for safe passage back to Portugal for all of us."

What was going on?

Anita stood up and brushed the dust off her knees. She took

a deep breath, opened the screen door, and stepped inside. She let the door slam, even though she knew never to do so. Anita didn't care.

"Mama, I got an 'A'…." She saw her parents huddled on the sofa. Their stressed expressions squashed Anita's excitement. Anita's father moved to stand next to the window with his back to the room.

She looked from her father to her mother. "Why is Papa home in the middle of the day?"

"Anita, come over here and sit down next to me." Her mother patted the space beside her on the sofa.

Anita slumped on the sofa and let her test fall to the floor. Something bad has happened. *Maybe Mama is going to have another baby. They would be excited to tell me the news. But no, that can't be it. They have frowns on their faces.*

Her mother looked at her husband, wrapped her arm around Anita, and kissed the top of her head. "Let me see your test, Anita." She held her hand out and waited for Anita to pick it up and hand it to her.

She gave Anita a weak smile and said, "This is very good, Anita. I am proud of you."

"Dominique." Sara looked over Anita's head at her husband. "She got an 'A' on her test. Aren't you proud of your daughter?" Dominique stared out the window but gave no reply. "Dominique, are you listening? Anita got an 'A' on her test." The statement hung in the air between them.

Anita was desperate to please her father. She wanted him to know she was smart and more intelligent than any boy in her class. But she knew he wouldn't let her know, even if he were proud. As a man, he couldn't show any emotion but anger.

She wanted to be a scientist. But opportunities to leave the village were few and practically nonexistent for girls. But that didn't sway her. It was the way African women lived in this place.

Dominique didn't turn to address either of them on the sofa. "Sara. It is fine that she is doing well in her studies, no matter the subject, but she is almost old enough to marry. She should focus on how to cook and clean. Her future is to make a suitable home for her husband and children."

Her father's crisp voice made Anita mad, but she knew not to show her emotions. She changed the topic. "What were you talking about when I came in?"

"Mind your own business, child!" her father said dismissively. He turned from the window, walked to the sofa, and towered over Anita. She shrank into the cushions with fear.

"Dominique!" Sara said. "Please don't speak to her that way. She was asking a simple question."

"She is 10! It doesn't involve her." He scowled and turned away.

Her mother patted Anita's arm. "Mama and Papa need to discuss something further. Go change from your school clothes and then take your brother outside to play until I call you."

"But I want to stay here," Anita protested. She received a stern look from both parents. Finally, she slid off the sofa and stomped to her room.

#

Dinner was late that night. Everyone except the two Belo children left the central playground to have dinner. Anita sat on a swing and debated whether she and her brother should go. She was hungry but didn't want to interrupt her parents again.

Should we wait until we are called in for dinner?

"I'm hungry," Anita's brother whined.

Little brothers. I can't wait to get away from you. She stopped the swing and stared at him. His eyes were watery, on the verge of tears. "I am, too. Come on. We are going home." She grabbed his arm and dragged him along so quickly that it was hard for him even to touch the ground. Dust billowed up as his feet shuffled along the ground.

"You're going too fast! And you're hurting my arm. I'm going to tell Dad." he whined again.

Anita stopped dead in her tracks and jerked him around to face her. She bent down and got nose-to-nose with him. "You'll do nothing of the kind. Do exactly what I tell you. Or I will tell them what you did to your stuffed animal." Her eyes were wide and fiery.

He cried, and she released her grip and hugged him. She knew she had to change his focus before they returned to the house, or she would be in trouble. "What is your favorite flavor of ice cream?" She wiped his face with her hand and noticed the excitement in his eyes.

"Are we going to have ice cream tonight?"

"I don't know. Let's go home and see what's what." She took his hand, and they walked slower and more comfortably. She smiled to herself. *Little brothers are so easily led.*

Their mother appeared on the road in front of them. "There you are. I am so glad I found you. It is late, and you must be hungry. Let's get you back and get some food in your tummy."

"Anita said we were going to have ice cream!"

Sara gave Anita a sideways glance. "Well, maybe not tonight, but soon."

"When Mama?" he asked.

"Soon." She ended the conversation, took him by the hand, and headed home. "Your father and I must talk to you both once we get home. Then you must eat, bathe, and get ready for bed."

Anita noticed her mother pause at the door and take a deep

breath before she stepped into the hot kitchen.

Their father sat at the table, newspaper in hand. "I am waiting for dinner."

"Go wash your hands," Sara said over her shoulder to Anita and her brother as she grabbed the pan and served the night's dinner.

Sara started the conversation once they were all at the table. "Your father is going to Uganda to work on a monkey farm. He will learn how to be a monkey handler." She gave a weak smile to her children. "As a handler, he will travel with the monkeys and care for them. It is a wonderful opportunity for him and our family. He will be gone for at least a year, maybe longer. In the meantime, he will send back the money to us, and I will return to teaching school. We will all have to sacrifice. Do you have questions?" She finished her speech, and everyone was silent.

What was there to say?

"We're going to have ice cream now?"

Anita poked her little brother's leg under the table. "Ouch, that hurt." He whined and swatted back at Anita.

"Anita, leave your brother alone," Sara said, annoyed with her children's behavior.

"But he started it...." She stopped her defense when she saw the anger in her mother's eyes. Instead, Anita answered Sara's question. "No, I don't think I have questions." Then Anita paused and looked at her father. "Wait, I have one. When are you leaving?"

Her father shot Anita a foul look in response to the forbidden question. Still, in a calm, distant voice, he said, "I leave the day after tomorrow." He grabbed the paper, rustled it open, and resumed his reading. *It was the end of the discussion.*

That night, Anita lay in bed and listened to the bugs' songs outside. She tossed and turned and fought her excitement about her father's departure. She loved her father, but she didn't like him. He always pointed out that he was correct. But on the other hand, he was mean and sometimes scared her.

And I scare my little brother.

Many in the village remarked how similar Dominique and Anita were in looks, intelligence, and stubbornness. It was a comparison Anita didn't like. As a result, she spent a lot of time and effort to exist outside her father's shadow. And she knew she wouldn't be just a housewife. That wasn't her purpose in life. She would be somebody. She didn't need his approval.

2: Dominique

October 1, 1967 - EN 100 Highway, Mocamedes Desert, Angola

Almost a year after his departure, Dominique was on his way home to his family. He'd hoped to bring back an opportunity for a better life. But all he had was an empty sack, a half-eaten sandwich, and a couple of German coins. Despite the situation, he was still excited to see his children and beautiful Sara. Most of all, Dominique was thrilled not to be mixed up in that craziness in Germany. He was lucky he'd made it out alive.

He squirmed in his bus seat and thought about what had gone wrong. The load of monkeys should have been stopped before it left Uganda. But none of the handlers spoke of concerns. Instead, they all feared for their lives as much as the monkeys did, which explained the strong bond the animals and handlers had with each other. He wiggled again in his seat, and a coin fell out of his pocket. Dominique didn't bother to retrieve it.

A fellow passenger leaned over. "Sir, you dropped a coin."

Dominique responded without a look. "It doesn't matter. I can't spend it where I am going, anyway."

The passenger shrugged, grabbed the coin, and put it in his pocket. Dominique gave a sideways glance, disgusted. He closed his eyes and hummed. Soon, he fell asleep, but it wasn't restful. The groan of the bus's dusty engine, the old shocks, and his body smell kept him from a peaceful sleep.

He dreamed about Sara, naked in their bed. She welcomed him home with open arms. He undressed and climbed on top of her. He had waited so long for this moment. But then the dream morphed, and Sara had him in a chokehold. In the background, a siren wailed.

Dominique screamed, and he was suddenly awake with his arms over his head, disoriented. His heartbeat quickly, and he panted. Then, he refocused on his surroundings and relaxed his arms.

Where was the siren?

He looked out the bus window and saw a dust storm brewing. It was the source of the sound. The passengers closed the windows and covered them with what they had to protect themselves from the fine dust.

The dust rolled in, but it seeped like fog, not a giant wave. The bus driver pushed on and focused on the road through scratches carved into the windshield by dust and dry windshield wipers. Everyone was on guard, and the baseline chatter on the bus fell silent. Things hid in the dust.

A hush took over the bus, and Dominique felt himself fall asleep again. He woke to a shove from his fellow seatmate. "Wake up. The busman says this is your stop."

He gathered his bags and stumbled to the front of the bus. The bus driver glared and huffed as Dominique stepped off the bus. Dominique turned to thank him, but the driver closed the door and sped off. He looked around. He had arrived. Destination, nowhere.

A layer of reddish-tan dust covered everything after the dust storm passed. The roads, buildings, and people were red, contrasted with the crisp blue sky. The scene was beautiful if you didn't have to live in it. Dominique opened his mouth to breathe and got the joy of tasting dirt. *Germany hadn't been like this, and neither had been Uganda.*

He started on foot towards his home. If he kept up his pace, he would be home by nightfall. The recent past was like a dream that had turned into a nightmare. He shook off the thought. There would be another opportunity, he was sure. What was the saying? "When one door closes, a window will open"?

It was something like that.

#

As the sun fell, he came to the village. He stopped and marveled at the sky's beautiful blaze of pink, orange, and yellow, in stark contrast to the ground as it took on dark and dirty shadows. He continued. His home was at the far end of the village. As he wandered through, he noticed not much had changed since he had been gone.

Had it really been a year?

The closer Dominique got to home, the more excited he was. As he walked, he waved to villagers as he passed on the streets. They did the same but with caution. He found that odd but shrugged it off as being surprised to see him. He passed buildings where evening lights flickered from the open windows. Typically, a warm invitation to come in, but Dominique quickened his pace. Soon, he would be secure in the comfort of his home.

Dominique stopped just outside his home. He could hear his children's chatter and saw Sara making dinner. Maybe it was one of his favorite meals. A wave of regret washed over him. No, it wouldn't be. He hadn't let Sara know he was coming back. That decision was another mistake in a long series of bad choices. He wanted to end the entire experience and the streak. But tomorrow was a new day, and he was home.

He dropped his suitcase and sack outside and charged into the kitchen with his arms open. "I'm back!"

Everyone froze—Sara was at the sink, and the kids were at the table. Dominique went to Sara. He leaned down and kissed her on the lips. He saw her eyes well up as she reached and placed her palms on his cheeks.

"Dominique, is that really you?" Sara asked.

"I am home now." He leaned in again for another kiss.

#

Dominique was surprised at how difficult it was to integrate back into village life. It felt strange to him. His daughter was different. She no longer took his direction; even his little boy seemed more independent. Sara seemed distant, even though she had made love to him. His fellow villagers were also reserved around him. He had left an elder, and now they treated him like a stranger.

Maybe everyone was better off without him.

#

The changes at home continued. Sara became moody. Was it punishment for his long absence? He knew it was hard for her. But he also noticed differences in how she interacted with the children. She was often short with them for no apparent reason, yet other times, she acted so full of love, like herself.

Maybe she was going through 'the change.'

The idea made no sense. Sara was still young, and they wanted more children. Dominique watched his beloved wife's temper grew shorter with the family, and she didn't sleep peacefully. She didn't eat, and she threw up afterward when she did. Finally, Dominique gave in and called the doctor.

Maybe she was already pregnant.

The doctor arrived sheathed in a mask and gloves. "What is the meaning of this?" Dominique pointed to the doctor's protective gear.

The doctor didn't respond. Instead, he took Sara into the bedroom and examined her. Dominique followed, sat in the corner, and watched.

The exam was short. Too short.

The doctor's head bowed, and he spoke in a quiet but authoritative tone, "Your wife is sick, Mr. Belo."

Dominique shot back, "I know that. That is why I called for you."

"She has The Fever."

Sara howled and cupped her face with her hands. Dominique jumped up from the chair and charged the doctor.

The doctor stopped him with one hand. "Mr. Belo, this situation is no one's fault. 'The Fever' is spreading through the countryside. So, eventually, it had to arrive here."

Dominique leaned close to the doctor's face. "Fix her!" His ears burned, and he felt blood rush inside his head.

The doctor took a step back. "I understand your fear and want her to be well again. She is a fine woman...." Dominique shot the doctor a look of defensiveness, but the doctor ignored him. "But Mr. Belo, I am afraid to tell you, there is no cure."

Sara wailed again. Dominique sat next to her and wrapped his arms around her. He rocked, hoping her panic would settle.

"What do you mean there's no cure? No cure *here*?" He pointed down at the ground and stomped his foot. "We'll travel wherever we need to go to make her well."

"No. You don't seem to understand. There is no cure anywhere. Sara could be very contagious to your whole family." The doctor stepped away from the couple. He continued to talk, yet no one listened. Dominique refocused when he heard the doctor say, "The best thing for you, your children, and the entire village would be to send Sara away and let her die in peace without infecting others."

Dominique leaped up and grabbed the doctor by the throat. "What do you mean, send her away?"

"Dominique, let the doctor go!" Sara shrilled.

The children stood in the doorway and watched. While their father still held the doctor, Sara tried to pull Dominique away. Everyone's screams filled the room with panic. Then, finally, the doctor broke free and ran out of the house.

3: Anita

October 19, 1967

Over the next two weeks, Anita watched her mother get sicker. The disease that invaded Sara's body turned her from a beautiful woman, full of confidence and kindness, to a human shell. Anita saw the physical transformation and sensed signs that The Fever also stripped Sara of her mind. Her mother became paranoid and angry, especially at night.

After dark, Sara would start arguments with Dominique over minor subjects. The words she would hurl at him made little sense, and in response, Anita's father would say nothing. Instead, he let her scream until she tired herself and fell asleep.

Sara's screams grew louder each night, and she hit Dominique when he tried to calm her. Anita and her brother sought cover in the bedroom closet while the nightly abuse occurred. This woman was no longer her mother, and Anita wished her dead.

Anita didn't understand why her father was so stubborn. The doctor had recommended that her mother be sent away or quarantined, but her father refused. Sara begged to leave for the children's sake, but Dominique refused.

It wasn't just Sara who was sick. Throughout the village, Anita saw others just as ill. She overheard talk that the disease they now called Bat Crap Fever ran rampant throughout the country, and there was talk of this being the next plague.

In response, the government deployed the military to regain control and stop the mass insanity that gripped the citizens throughout Angola. It hadn't worked. The military presence, dressed in gas masks, didn't calm the people down but instead added to the hysteria. As a child, all Anita could do was watch and hope the disease wouldn't come for her.

#

Anita looked at her mother as she sat on the sofa. Sara's eyes were glazed, and she clawed at her skin. Dominique sat in his chair and read his newspaper.

How can Papa be so clueless about Mama's feelings?

Anita leaned toward her brother. "Come. It's time to get in the closet."

For once, he didn't question. Instead, he slowly stood and inched his way out with Anita. They settled on the closet floor, surrounded by boxes, as their mother stomped into the bedroom.

"Where are those kids?" Sara screamed.

Anita jumped at the tone of her mother's voice. She cried in silence. Her mother's voice grew louder. Anita wrapped her arms around her brother and rocked as she repeated, "Stop! Just stop."

"Sara, calm down," said Dominique. "I am sure they are somewhere around."

Anita pushed a louver and saw her father look around the room for the children. Anita felt anger toward her father for his breezy attitude about the situation.

Dominique continued to try to reason with her. "Besides, you're in no condition to be around them. So, it would be best if you calmed down. You are scaring them."

"Scaring them?" Sara repeated as she collapsed on the bed. When she spoke next, her voice was small. "I'm scared too. My body is betraying me, and I don't even know how I got this disease." She wiped the tears away from her cheeks.

Dominique sat next to her on the bed and held her hand. "I have something to tell you."

Anita held her breath and tightened her grip on her brother.

"This Bat Crap Fever virus, the Marburg virus, I saw it in the lab in Germany. Marburg, Germany."

Anita watched the scene. She saw her mother's face turn red and her eyebrows furrowed. Anita knew that meant Sara was mad. Anita bit down on her anger and the need to scream at her father.

"I didn't even know you went to Germany. Why? When? How did you get to Germany?" Sara's voice squeaked.

He ignored her questions and continued. "There was an accident in the lab."

"What accident? What lab? What are you talking about?"

"I heard the virus was named after the place it first appeared...." He wrapped his arm around her and held her close. "I put two and two together and..." Dominique shook his head. "I thought I escaped."

Anita could see her mother's eyes narrow as she pushed against Dominique. She broke free from his hold and shifted from him on the bed.

He hung his head. "Maybe the sickness followed me."

Sara jumped off the bed. "What the hell were you thinking? You jeopardized the safety of your whole family! And for what, a couple of Kwanzas?"

"Deutsche Marks."

"What?"

Dominique raised his face to look at her, her eyes fiery red. A trail of blood seeped from her nostril.

"Deutsche Marks. They paid me in Deutsche Marks. That's the currency in Germany." His voice was flat.

"You did this to me! Is that why you never fought back? Is that why you just let me go on my nightly rampages? Did you figure one night soon I would die anyway, so why bother telling me? Or is it because you're a coward?"

Sara stood with her hands clenched as the fever boiled her blood. Her body looked like a wood nugget in a well-stoked fire. Sara charged Dominique, and Anita covered her mouth to stifle a scream.

Sara was a foot shorter and a hundred pounds lighter, but she pushed Dominique hard, and he fell against the door. His head slammed into the door hinge, and he stumbled forward, arms extended.

Sara grabbed a broom and smacked his head across his ear. He held his arms up in defense of another blow to the head. Sara poked low and hit the top of his kneecap with the butt of the broom handle. His legs buckled, and he landed in a prayer position on both knees.

"Sara, please. I didn't know I carried the disease out of the lab. I was careful. And I didn't know that it doesn't have a cure. Please, Sara. I will do anything. What can I do? I'm sorry. I went to Uganda and Germany for you and the children...."

Sara moved to the side of him. He bent down low, forearms and forehead on the floor, and muttered. "I'm so sorry."

Sara raised her left shoe and stomped on Dominique's neck. Anita covered her mouth with both hands, but it wasn't enough. Her screams were still apparent. Soon, Anita's brother joined in with his cries. He flailed his hands, and the clothes tangled him like a giant spider web.

A bang on the bedroom door stopped Anita's screams. She lifted the louver and peered into the bloody face of her mother.

Another pound and Sara grunted in response to the noise. She stepped towards Anita's hiding place as the bedroom door split open, and a rush of military men flooded the room with drawn guns. Sara grunted, swung around, and dove for the men over the bed. They responded with gunshots, and Sara fell face-first on the bed.

The men surrounded the bed, guns trained on Sara. Anita rushed out of the closet into the men's legs. She crawled onto the bed beside her mother and tried to cradle her head. "I'm sorry, Mama, for wanting you dead. Please, Mama, come back. Come back!"

She held her face close to her mother's and looked for life, but she only saw a vacant stare. Sara was dead. Anita felt herself being pulled away from the body on the bed.

"Are you crazy like your mother? You can get infected by touching her body! Do you want to get sick like your mother?"

The military man put his face, almost black from the sun, close to Anita's and stared. His eyes showed no empathy for Anita. He scared her. Finally, he broke the gaze between them, and she slid down on the floor next to the bed.

One officer checked for Domonique's pulse, looked up, and shook his head. He then stood and checked Sara's pulse. He shook his head again. Anita closed her eyes, and she rocked back and forth.

The commander announced, "Mission accomplished. Move out." The men filed out, and the children were alone in an airy silence of death.

Anita looked up to see her brother as he stood before her. He reached for her, and when she didn't move, he knelt beside her. He stroked her hair like she had taught him to do with kittens. She looked at his tear-stained face and saw his vacant eyes. He was only six. He was too young to understand what had happened. She feared he wouldn't be the same ever again. She reached up and palmed his face.

It's just you and me now.

4: Anita

October 30, 1967

Anita and her brother endured days of tests by the World Health Organization (WHO). She didn't understand what they looked for in the results. So, to protect her brother and herself, Anita made it a point to eavesdrop on conversations the head research doctor had with his colleagues. She and others in the village had developed antibodies for the Marburg Virus. She wasn't sure how that happened, but it was her ticket out of Angola.

It happened so quickly. One day, she played outside. The next, her parents died, and she and her brother were lab rats. She could hear her mother's voice, "Make the best of the situation." Anita's shock subsided, and she replaced it with anger. *It was all Papa's fault.* Mama didn't have to die. But each time she thought about it, she reminded herself there wasn't a cure.

Her mother would still be alive if she hadn't been so dependent on her father. She vowed never to be in the same predicament. No man would provide for her. Instead, she would dedicate her own life to a cure, with no help needed from others.

She didn't want to leave Angola, but she was only 11, an orphan, and the decision wasn't hers. She protested, but in her heart, she knew she had to go. It was for their safety. Anita accepted the decision and vowed to come back and save her countrymen and women.

Dr. Burger from the WHO offered an opportunity to move to Germany. It was a lifeline out of the hell her village had become. So many would die from starvation or civil war if not from the fever. There was no future in Angola. It was best to get out of the country and to a place where she could grow up and study to be a scientist. Still, she had reservations about the move.

Germany. Isn't that where Papa had been?

"You're going to live in Germany now." Dr. Burger crouched down to Anita's level.

"Why?" she asked.

Dr. Burger stood to his full height, placed his hands on his hips, and peered down at her through ice-blue eyes. "Because I think you have the key to solving this mystery. Pack your suitcase so that we can leave."

Anita stood in the middle of her room and wondered what to pack. She wanted to take it all.

He brushed a hand through his white hair and yelled, "Quickly!"

Anita jumped, and the tears rolled down her cheeks.

"Shush. Crying is a useless reaction to stress." Dr. Burger pushed her aside and shoved a few clothes into the bag. Anita howled. "Oh, forget it. Take what you like. Whether it is a toy, family heirlooms, or a set of clothes, it doesn't matter. You both will get new items in Germany. Quick, now. Do what I say."

Anita obeyed, grabbed her favorite toy, a doll and a dress, and placed them gingerly in the suitcase. She had already hidden her father's letters from Uganda and Germany in the bag's lining. She didn't know if they were significant, but she didn't want Dr. Burger to keep or destroy them. They might come in handy. She had a dark feeling that Dr. Burger and his team wouldn't find a cure.

It was up to her. She understood the ins and outs of Angolan life, and the foreign white man did not. That was her secret weapon.

But now, she couldn't help herself. She cried. Just this one time was all she would allow herself. She would never lose control over her emotions again. She wiped the tears from her cheeks, closed the bag, and said goodbye to her life in Angola.

Part 2

5: Anita

May 19, 2017 - Fairview University, Charlotte, North Carolina

Over 40 years. I have spent four decades on the cure, and now it is being taken away!

The deep voice of the Dean of Graduate Studies interrupted Anita's thoughts. "It isn't as if we are firing you, Anita. We are just refusing to give you another extension on your dissertation."

The office they met in was stuffy and mirrored how Anita felt. Dean Hasselbach leaned back in a tufted brown leather chair behind a large oak desk. The bright sun shone through the leaded glass window and placed the Dean's facial expressions in shadow. Anita sat, speechless, in a faded flame-stitched fabric wing chair with threadbare arms.

She kept still and stared at nothing as she tried to hold back the flood of emotions. She rubbed the chair's arms and realized from their look that she wasn't the first. The thought made her stop. She never wanted to be lumped in with "normal" people.

She stuffed her anger down before she spoke. "I am doing good work here. When I discover the cure, it will bring a lot of press and money to this university." This statement sounded a little too desperate for Anita. She hated the needy tone of her voice.

Without acknowledgment, the Dean continued to drone on.

"Frankly, we have seen little progress. The Graduate Studies Committee discussed the situation at length. Ultimately, we all agreed that this was the best course of action. If you read the Doctoral Agreement, you will see we are well within our rights to take this approach."

As the Dean talked, Anita busied herself, processing the problem and coming up with a solution. Her anger grew. *How dare they do this to me?* She was tired of the Dean's speech. "I don't give a crap about your paperwork. I want my job back, and I deserve it."

The Dean narrowed his eyes but kept his tone even. "Anita, please. I was trying to say we have also agreed to keep you on as a professor if you so choose. You are still one of our best researchers, and I think you have much to offer undergraduate biology students." He paused and tilted his chair again with an air of dominance and dismissal.

He clasped his hands together to form the clichéd thinking triangle. "The job is yours if you want it."

Anita shifted in her chair. She could make the job work. It was a crappy job, but she still would have access to the lab. And her quest could continue. She needed to talk to Roger and get his opinion. She tried hard to focus on the Dean as he sat across from her. He said all the diplomatic things, but she knew he was tired of her.

Ass. Enjoy your moment of glory. You can't get rid of me that easily.

She grew impatient and didn't want to wait for Roger's opinion. She faked an interested and gracious response. "Yes, I think I'll take the job. When does it start?"

"You can start with the summer session. I recommend contacting Dr. Spivey for the course syllabus and student roster."

The Dean let the chair snap forward into its upright position and stood to signal the end of the meeting. He walked around the desk and met Anita at the door. He extended his hand and said, "I believe in Alexander Graham Bell's quote, 'When one door closes, another opens.' So, I am saying goodbye to a doctoral student and hello to a talented professor. Welcome aboard."

Anita barely touched his hand as she shook, turned, and left the office.

The Dean called after her as she walked away, "The best thing would be to clear out your possessions from the lab. Do you need help? I can call campus security."

In a dismissive tone, Anita looked over her shoulder and said, "No, there's nothing of importance there."

It was the truth. Anita was uncomfortable with displays of her personal life at work. Was that because she didn't have a personal life? This made her mad, and she completed the journey back to the lab in more of a stomp than a walk.

#

Calmed by the walk back to the lab, she inserted her key and was grateful they hadn't changed the lock. Anita slipped in, and the familiar smell of the lab welcomed her like a warm hug. She sat on a lab stool, stunned by what had just happened. A half hour ago, this was her lab. Now, it was up for grabs for the next golden child of the university. Her chest expanded and contracted, but she couldn't catch enough air. The tears flowed down her face like the emotions stirring in her head. Her mood changed from sadness to anger toward herself. Loss of control and tears wouldn't help the situation.

Damn you, Dean Hasselbach!

She grabbed her phone and dialed Roger. He answered on the second ring. "Hello, Anita."

"They canned me," she blurted out her reply to his greeting.

"What are you talking about?"

"The Advisor Council stopped me from going forward with

my doctorate."

"Can they do that?"

"Apparently, I signed some bogus agreement. Who the hell knows? That was ten years ago."

There was a long pause before Roger asked, "So, where to next?"

Anita pulled the phone away from her ear and stared at it. *What a strange question.* She paced. "What do you mean, go next? We aren't going anywhere." Then, she heard glass breaking in the background and stopped in her tracks. "Roger?"

"Shit," he said.

"Did something break? What are you doing?" She didn't wait for his response and continued to pace. "Roger, we aren't going anywhere. They have offered me a professor's position, and I am taking it. I just need a plan to do my research on the side."

"So, you will still have the lab?"

"Access to it, but the lab and office are no longer only mine. I share it with two other professors. But I have a job."

"Are you okay with that?"

"You sound distant. What are you doing?"

"I just spilled something. Go on."

"I guess, all things considered, this is the best scenario." Anita tapped her lips with her finger. "I might have more time to dedicate to finding a cure because I won't be bogged down with the dissertation. And access to a pool of undergrads who are more than willing to help me. Oh, maybe I can get rid of Kerri now."

"Kerri is not your enemy," Roger said under his breath.

Anita stopped her pace around the room again. "What? Never mind. Did I mention I will teach biology? Roger, thank you so much for listening to me. This has really helped. I will let you go now. I will see you in a little while." Anita hung up without Roger's response.

6: Roger

May 19, 2017 - Robbins Meadow Neighborhood, Charlotte, North Carolina

Roger stared at the phone. It was his turn to be stunned. Roger stared at the broken glass he had just smashed on the kitchen counter. Vodka had spilled over the front of his dress shirt and tie. His head spun. Maybe he could convince Anita to leave Charlotte after all. The idea sparked a whirlwind of ideas for Roger.

Yes, this was the opportunity he had wanted.

Roger poured himself a drink to celebrate the thought. He looked around the 1970's kitchen. He had always hated this kitchen. They had never updated in hopes of not being here long. But three years had turned into ten, and the damn room was just as nasty as it was the day they moved in. If they stayed, things would have to change. The kitchen was an excellent place to start. He poured himself another drink and headed upstairs to change his wet clothes.

#

Roger had made some decisions by the time Anita got home two hours later. He wouldn't reveal most of his plans because they didn't include her. Or was it because she would try to convince him to change his mind? He couldn't decide. It didn't matter. For now, they were his secrets. He wanted to take control of his life, and he felt strong.

The back door opened, and Anita appeared like the Tasmanian devil. Roger threw her a smile as he stirred a pot of sauce. He had already made a batch of Klapperys, a type of fudge, and one of Anita's favorites. "I was just starting the pasta."

"It smells wonderful in here." Anita threw her day bag on the table. "I thought of going out for dinner. But with the smell of fudge and that sauce, I am excited to stay in. I'm not going anywhere."

Anita sat down at the kitchen table and watched Roger work. "I would like to help."

"No, you're good. I've got it."

"I am going to make myself a drink. Would you like me to freshen up yours?"

"That would be nice," Roger said without turning his head.

Avoid eye contact with her. It was his first attempt to create a separation between them. It was a simple task, but it was a challenge to execute. She knew how to read his mind, especially when she looked into his eyes.

"After I hung up with you, I met with Dr. Spivey," she said while she took his glass, filled it with vodka, and replaced it on the counter in arm's reach. Roger acknowledged the glass with a nod of his chin and continued to chop the vegetables.

Anita sat. "He says he is glad to have me on board and that I may become a vital part of his master plan for the biology department. Did you know he just took over the Dean's position from Dr. Hamilton? I didn't. I'm not sure why I didn't know that." She shrugged at the question. "Anyway, I guess I have been in a fog with the dissertation and research."

Roger gave a head shake in agreement.

She continued to drone on with her monolog. "So the class

I will teach over the summer is a Biology 101 segment. It will be a piece of cake and allow me to regroup. I asked Dr. Spivey how much access I would have to the labs, and he seemed quite surprised by the question. He saw no reason not to have access, so it's business as usual. If I have the approval of my new boss, whose business is it to ask what I am doing there?"

You talk at me, not to me. Most times, you don't even realize I am here.

Roger asked, "Did you tell Dr. Spivey that you were continuing the research for the cure?" He struggled to sound interested.

"Well, not exactly. It was more of a wink-and-nudge moment. Once I have the cure, the university will have to grovel at my feet to keep me and the cure so they can profit from it. We both know they only worry about the bottom line." She drained her glass.

Roger had already finished his drink. "Would you like another?" He held up the bottle, and she nodded. He refreshed both and went back to work.

"I love you, Roger. I'm not sure what I would do without you," she blurted out.

He turned slowly, and Anita stared into her glass as she swirled the liquid. *She rarely said I love you,* and tonight, it seemed even more uncomfortable now that he wanted to leave her. He wondered if she sensed it. *Why else would she say it?*

She changed the subject. "Do you think it is too late in the season to plant out front?"

She got up, opened the silverware drawer, and took out utensils for dinner. "Are we going to eat here or in the dining room?" She didn't wait for a response and went and set the dining table.

Roger answered her first question. "That would be good for you. You have always wanted to do some gardening."

She smiled. "Maybe I can ask the neighbor for help. Bailey always has such a pretty front slope area. I asked her once about what she was planting because there seemed to be no maintenance, but now that I will have extra time on my hands." Anita grabbed cloth napkins and added, "Yes, I will try to catch her the next time she is out front."

Roger piped in, "Maybe you can ask about that tree. You can find out if they will do something with it soon," He grimaced. That tree had done too much damage to their house during Hurricane Harry, and he was still worried about it when the winds were strong.

Anita came back into the kitchen. "Maybe after dinner, I can come with you on your walk. See what the other neighbors are doing in their front yards?"

"No!" Roger whirled around.

"Why not?"

"Because I like to walk alone." He saw Anita's face and realized he had offended her. "It will be dark by the time I head out. So, you won't see much. Maybe we will go for a walk this weekend." He turned away.

She came up behind him, looped her arms under his, hugged him from behind, and rested her head on his shoulder. "Roger, you're the best."

Roger fought the urge to shudder and broke the embrace. "Let's eat."

7: Anita

May 20, 2017

Though Anita kept access to the research labs, she had to vacate the office she had occupied for ten years. The lab was cleared out yesterday, but she tackled her office on a Saturday when most other researchers weren't around.

The rumor mill buzzed the second she left the Dean's office yesterday. She had made peace with the university's decision. However, she still didn't like the idea of face-to-face encounters with her so-called colleagues. She would eventually set the story straight, but now she couldn't deal with others. Anita hadn't in the past. *Why start now?*

Anita told herself this as the elevator doors opened, and she entered an empty hall. Then, after she looked both ways, she darted to the office door. A rush of heat ran from her stomach to her cheeks as yesterday's conversation replayed in her head. She fiddled with the keys and damned herself for the open wound of the situation to fuel her negative emotions.

You need to play nice to continue your research.

The latch on the lock released, and she slipped into the office. She softly closed the door and leaned on the door frame to survey the room. *Where to start? Why did I collect so much stuff?*

The sunshine on this May afternoon was bright. It lit up the room and exposed dust that hung in the air. The days were still relatively free from humidity, so she opened the window for some fresh air. She could hear the chatter of students below as they soaked up the sun and tried to cram for finals.

Anita started with her bookshelf, pulled out a pile of dusty journals from her earlier research, and placed the stacks on the desk. She sat and opened the one labeled, "History of the Marburg Virus: A Hemorrhagic Fever / Bat Crap Fever."

General History Notes: 1950–Lake Victoria, Uganda

Lake Victoria Mango Fruit Orchard was owned and operated by a British Company, London Industries, Falmouth, England (LIFE). The farmland was 50 acres and had approximately 4000 fruit trees planted in 1925. The location promised the mango orchard would perform well for many decades. In addition, it had access to water on the banks of Lake Victoria and diverse opportunities for nurturance from the local area's array of decayed flora and fauna.

The parent company (LIFE) invested 10,000 British Pounds to improve the farm with soil, fertilization, irrigation, and employee training. After ten unsuccessful growing seasons, the trees showed no recorded improvement.

The fruit grew but did not meet industry standards. The mature fruit weighed only 50 grams, whereas the average mango was 200 to 210 grams. Their skins were thick and waxy, and the flesh was pale yellow and grainy. In 1960, the company abandoned the orchard and left the fruit to rot.

In 1963, LIFE sold the land and the trees to a local Uganda company, Tumbili Industries (TI). However, in reality, TI was a shell company of LIFE. TI razed 90%/3600 trees to make room for a new monkey farm. The remaining trees were protected during construction and provided much-needed shade for the new structure and a place for the monkeys to exercise.

The monkey farm opened for business in 1965 after three delays in the construction process. Local officials listed unsatisfactory sewer and drainage design issues as the cause of the delay. First-hand accounts (all interviewees refused to give their names for fear of the consequences) stated there was no construction design, plan, or oversight. As a result, the raw sewage (from the monkeys and farm workers) ran off into Lake Victoria.

After opening, witnesses observed widespread neglect of the monkeys. TI required a three-week turnaround to complete orders for monkeys used as lab test subjects. Only when an order was placed did the farm operators feed the monkeys regularly. After three weeks, the monkeys would be ready to ship. They would appear to be in satisfactory condition for travel and delivery.

In between requests, the operators left the monkeys to their own devices. The monkeys spent most of their time hunting for food on the farm and hiding in the remaining mango trees. The mango trees were still producing fruit, becoming the central portion of the monkey's diet.

Anita stopped reading. She knew what came next and hesitated. It would open old wounds from her childhood. A chill ran up her spine. The temperature in the room had cooled as the sun set. She rubbed her face and switched on the desk lamp. She sat back in the chair and gazed at the office. There wasn't anything other than the journals she wanted.

Screw it. Let the cleaning people clear this mess. I'm no one's maid.

Anita got up, closed the window, and placed two moving boxes on the desk. She pulled down the rest of her journals and packed them. She opened the filing cabinet next, grabbed a handful of hanging folders, and shoved them in boxes. I'll sort them at home. In the end, she had six boxes. She was surprised that she had gathered so much stuff.

How to get them to the car?

Anita was interrupted by a knock on the door. A man opened the door and stuck his head in. "Oh hey, Professor Belo, I saw the light on and thought I should check on it." He was tall and blond, with blue eyes and broad shoulders. He wasn't one of her favorite colleagues, but he could help with the boxes in a pinch.

"Josh, so glad you came by. I'm cleaning out the office, and you stopped by just in time to help me get these boxes to my car." She said it in a way that he couldn't refuse.

Anita noted Josh's reaction. He gazed at his feet as he shuffled them back and forth. She had made him feel uncomfortable. *Good.* There was a fine line between being served and being the server. Anita always wanted to be served. Anita and Roger always did. She turned away before he could protest.

Josh reluctantly said, "Sure, I can help. I'll get the cart from the storage room." Josh disappeared down the hall.

8: Bailey

July 19, 2017 - Robbins Meadow Neighborhood, Charlotte, North Carolina

Bailey Carroll stood on South James Road in front of her house and surveyed the damage the freak windstorm had done to her front slope plantings. It wasn't what she wanted to be doing on her Saturday morning in July. It was 8:00 a.m., and the heat from the sun was already unbearable. She wiped the sweat off her forehead with the back of her hand and left a streak of mud. She sighed as she bent over and attacked the broken twigs of her Russian Sage.

Yardwork isn't fun or glamorous.

"You wanted a house and yard, Bailey. Stop complaining and get it done," she said out loud. She looked at her dog, Alex, as he slept under the Japanese maple's shade. "Nice life, if you can get it." She was in a foul mood, and being on display in the front yard didn't help matters. The scrappy terrier mutt raised and barked once to break Bailey's rant. She looked around to see the cause of the dog's attention and noticed Roger, the next-door neighbor, in his car.

"Alex, it's okay. Go back to sleep. Some supervisor you are." The dog complied and lowered his head again with a sigh.

Why is Roger just sitting there?

Bailey willed herself to continue her work, even though she

felt self-conscious. She tried to steal a glimpse of him without being too obvious. Roger creeped Bailey out. She couldn't put her finger on it if anyone pressed her for a reason. He just did. Maybe it was because she'd seen him lurk around the neighborhood after dark several times. He would stop and stare at her house for several minutes for no apparent reason.

Bailey moved the trash barrel along the front to the next plant that needed attention. Alex raised his head and barked again, but a tail wag accompanied it this time.

Helen is on her way over.

Helen Platte, the across-street neighbor, was in her late seventies but looked like she was still in her fifties. Bailey hoped she would look that good at that age. Helen was a bit of a gossip and was a good distraction while Bailey weeded; today, Bailey welcomed the distraction.

"That was some storm last night, wasn't it?" Helen said as she crossed the street.

Bailey smiled. "We weren't here. We were at a networking event."

"Well, it got real dark, and the wind picked up. I was afraid we would see a cow fly by!" She laughed at her joke. She breezed by Bailey to greet Alex under the tree, and Bailey followed.

"It did a number on the fence." Bailey pointed in the general direction of the backyard. "Jordan is working on it right now, trying to make it secure again."

Helen patted the top of Alex's head. "Does he need help? I could send the Mister over."

"Ah, I don't think so. Thanks for the offer."

Helen changed the subject. "Why is Roger sitting in his car? Must be hotter than hell in there." She let her eyes roll and nodded her chin over her shoulder.

"I have no idea. He's been there for a while."

"He's…" Helen stopped herself and bit her lip. "He's weird," she said abruptly.

Bailey laughed. "I think we established that a while ago. By the way, did you see Anita cornered me a month ago while I was out here?" Bailey took a big swig of water from her travel mug.

"Good God, what for?"

"She wanted to know what I had planted. She told me it was high time to get her front to look like mine."

It was Helen's turn to laugh. "As if! They have lived here for over ten years and can barely manage to have the lawn mowed." She shook her head. "That poor old man they have coming to do the lawn. And then they nitpick his work."

"That's exactly what I thought…." Bailey stopped in mid-sentence. "Speak of the devil."

They both turned to see Anita as she approached them. Alex stood and barked without a tail wag. Helen patted Alex's head to calm him down while Bailey fed him a steady stream of treats. She handed the treats to Helen and went to meet Anita on the street.

Bailey looked over Anita's shoulder and noticed that Roger wasn't in his car anymore. "Good morning."

Anita didn't respond to the greeting. "I am glad to catch you upfront. My gardener is coming over to do some planting today."

So, what's your point?

Anita narrowed her eyes. "We had some limbs fall in our yard last night."

Bailey tried to plaster a smile on her face. "I'm sorry to hear that." Bailey saw a flicker of anger in Anita's eyes. She softened her tone and added, "Would you like Jordan to come over and pick them up?"

Anita huffed and shook her head just a little. "Well, no. I will have our guy do that." She hesitated before continuing, "I just wanted to reiterate that we think that tree is an insurance liability."

Bailey followed Anita's hand and eyes toward the 75-foot pecan between their two properties. Bailey's shoulders tensed, and she took a deep breath before she met Anita's gaze. Alex growled, and Bailey could hear Helen try to silence him.

Fuck. Not this again.

"As I said, I'm sorry some limbs came down. I will send Jordan over."

Anita cut Bailey off. "Roger and I agree. The tree should come down before it does more damage. In the hurricane of…"

Bailey snapped back, "That hurricane was before we moved in. We had an arborist look at the tree when we bought the house. The tree is fine." She kicked herself for being so snippy.

Play nice, Bailey.

Bailey locked eyes with Anita, and a shiver ran up her back. She wasn't sure who creeped her out more, Roger or Anita. She stood there and wondered why they always brought up that damn tree topic with her and not her husband, Jordan.

"As part of our yearly maintenance, we will have the tree guys recheck its health. Would that make you feel better?" Bailey's voice was thick with snark.

Anita gazed at the tree again. "For now."

Bailey hated that she and Anita weren't on good terms, but she felt that even if the tree weren't a source of friction, they wouldn't be close, not like she was with Helen. She tried to save face and changed the subject. "What are you going to plant?"

"What?" Anita's head still turned to the tree.

"You mentioned your lawn guy was coming today to plant." Bailey smiled and hoped it wasn't too fake.

Anita shifted her gaze back to Bailey. "You know what you recommended." She gave a weak smile in return. Then, she quickly turned and walked away. "Have to get ready for his arrival."

"Bye," Bailey said to Anita's back. She stood there and watched Anita climb her stairs and enter the house. *It's odd that they always have their blinds closed.*

"That was weird," Helen said. "Alex here thinks they are weird, too." She hugged the dog, and Alex licked her cheek.

"Weird is an understatement." Bailey turned back to Helen. "I want to finish this clean-up before she comes out again."

Helen stood up, patted Bailey on the shoulder, and headed back across the street. "Let me know if you need help with the fence," she said over her shoulder but didn't wait for a response.

Alex barked again and started to jump and wag his tail. Jordan walked up beside Bailey. "What did she want?"

"Who, Helen?"

"No. Anita."

"Guess." She gave her husband a little smirk. "She informed me that there were limbs in their backyard from yesterday's storm. Yet, another opportunity to bid for the tree removal."

"Oh man, I'll go over there and clean them up."

Bailey held her hand up. "She told me there was no need. Their lawn guy would do it."

"I'll be right back," Jordan said as he darted to the backyard.

Now that Bailey was alone again, she felt exposed. This wasn't a new feeling. She felt like she was on display whenever she did yardwork on the front slope. Of course, it was her front yard, but the entire community seemed to want to give her input on what she did. She didn't realize it would be this way when they bought the house. She turned to the slope and wondered how much longer she needed to be out there.

Stop bitching. You wanted this house.

Jordan reappeared in front of her. "The only limb I saw in their backyard is on the other side of the property. It looks like one from Mr. Huron's trees."

Bailey was surprised at how upset she was, and a tear fell from her eye and ran down her cheek. "Doesn't matter. It will always be our fault."

Professor Belo's journal entry:

Journal Entry: October 2, 2017

Scope– New Case Study Opened / Test for Marburg Hemorrhagic Fever

Identification–Patient Alpha 1

Appraisal–

Physical attributes– Fever, headache, chills, muscle pain.

Behaviors–Overall, not feeling well.

Patient Alpha 1 notes–Antibodies missing?

Analysis–Patient Alpha 1 exhibits symptoms aligned with the first generalization phase of the Marburg Hemorrhagic Fever.

Report–Specific testing is required due to the disease presenting itself in the same way as many other, more common viruses.

9: Anita

October 2, 2017

Anita couldn't shake the crappy feeling she had had for the last couple of weeks. She couldn't decide if it was the flu, menopause, or something else. Whatever it was, it hadn't responded to over-the-counter cold medicine, which worried her. She had been reluctant to do a blood test to give her more insight into her unease. Today, Anita felt on edge because she would soon have the answer, she hoped.

She paced the empty lab, and every time she passed by her computer, she looked to see if the results had been delivered. She huffed at the computer screen and resumed her roam around the room. As she moved, she ruminated.

Over ten years in this room, and one email might change everything.

She had taught her one class, Biology 101. Then, she spent the rest of her time in the lab. She was no longer a doctoral candidate. But her research for a cure for the Marburg Virus went on more covertly. It was what she expected when she accepted the deal three years ago.

The university took a "don't ask, don't tell" stance on the subject. They both knew there would be significant profit and recognition if Anita found a cure, a pure example of American capitalism at its finest. She was more than willing to exploit their greed.

The computer dinged, and she rushed over to the screen. There it was, the answer to her questions. She opened the email and previewed the attachment simultaneously as she sent the document to print.

No. No, no, no. It can't be!

Anita reread the results. The sample tested positive for Marburg Hemorrhagic Fever. The result was a death sentence. Her mind raced while her white sterile lab swirled around her, and the edges of her sight grew dark.

Anita ticked off the symptoms as she read: nausea, vomiting, chest pain, a sore throat, abdominal pain, diarrhea, weight loss, delirium, shock, liver failure, massive hemorrhaging, and multi-organ dysfunction. And then, death.

Panic crept up into her mouth, and she gagged on the bile. Though she felt lightheaded, her mind gave her only one thought: Get home now! She grabbed the results, stumbled into the vapor lock chamber, and clawed at her clean-room boilersuit. She successively freed herself from the protective equipment and pressed the button to engage the disinfectant spray. The outer door unlocked when the jet stopped, and the monitor sensed it was "all clear."

Anita ran face-first into her lab assistant, Kerri, in the hall. Kerri asked, "Are you okay? You look very pale."

Anita squinted at her assistant, unable to compute what she had said. Kerri's voice seemed muffled and distant. Anita's eyesight blurred. "I have to go!"

"Oh, you're not in any condition to go anywhere. You can't stand up straight. I don't think driving is a good idea. Come sit, and I will get you a glass of water." Kerri tugged on Anita's elbow, but she resisted.

"No. No, you don't understand. There's no more time. I have to go!" Anita shooed Kerri away and stormed down the hall.

She rested on the door handle at the front doors of the Science

Department building before she plunged through the doorway. A blast of stagnant fall air smacked her in the face and stuck in her throat. She didn't want to vomit, but she couldn't breathe. Anita tried to calm herself as she continued to gasp.

She needed to get home to Roger. Roger always comforted her, and he would know what to do next. Anita's breath slowed, and her nausea receded. With renewed strength, she straightened and headed to the parking garage. Her head continued to spin, and she wobbled as she walked.

Of course, groups of students would be in the courtyard between classes.

Anita dodged people along the path from the building to the parking deck. Focused on only one thing, she pushed aside a young man who was in her way as she passed.

"What the hell!" he said. He threw up his arms in disgust.

Anita didn't care, and she didn't stop. She had to get home.

Anita stopped in the garage's shade. It was dark and cool but only relieved her slightly from the Charlotte fall heat. As her eyes adjusted to the dim light, she searched for her car but couldn't remember where she'd parked. Frantic and nauseous again, Anita dug in her purse to locate her car keys. A tiny whimper escaped her lips when she found them. She extended her arm and pressed the car's fob to locate her vehicle.

Her hand shook while she fiddled with the keys to open the door. She damned herself for not getting the unlock button on her fob fixed. Finally, the door was open. She slid into the driver's seat and slammed the door shut. She screamed at the top of her lungs and pounded the steering wheel to release her panic.

Anita had dedicated her entire life to finding a cure for the Marburg Virus. Over the years, she had gone through countless failed clinical trials. *So why now?* Anita cried, even though she hated crying. It was a feeble reaction. But now, in peak stress, she felt differently.

A tap on the window shook her out of her thoughts, and she looked up to see two young men.

"Hey lady, are you okay?"

Anita wiped her face with her palms, alarmed by her loss of control. She refocused her attention on the men at her driver's side door. Her expression changed from dazed to angry. *What the hell do they want?* She ignored them.

They knocked again.

In her head, she screamed, *Go away!* But out loud, she cried, "NO, I am not! And it's none of your business!"

She turned the key, threw the gear into reverse, and screeched out of the parking space. The car lunged backward, and a cloud of tire smoke engulfed the Good Samaritans. Pleased with her exhibit, she jammed the car into drive and drove toward home.

The two men watched the black BMW station wagon as it sped away and shrugged. Then, one guy turned to the other. "Crazy bitch."

10: Roger

October 2, 2017

Roger disconnected a call with Kerri, Anita's lab assistant. A storm named Anita headed his way. He picked up his book to continue where he left off but was distracted. A heavy sigh escaped as he gazed at the page. It would have to wait. Once she was home, there would be no time for a good story. The sound of crushed gravel in the driveway alerted him to Anita's arrival. He set the book down and patted it like a beloved cat.

He picked up a letter he found stuck in the front door today. It was a notification of the neighbor's scheduled tree removal. Roger was relieved by the news, but it would have to wait. Roger skimmed the notice again before he slid it into his blazer's breast pocket.

Mug of tea in hand, he moved to the dining-room window to get a glimpse of Anita. His neck tensed as he prepared himself for Anita's mood. Roger had mixed emotions about Anita, and he always did. He loved her, but she was bossy and stubborn, traits in overdrive from what Kerri described.

Roger's loving side was relieved to see she had gotten home. On a good day, Anita ran red lights and rolled through stop signs, but today… The world was lucky she had done no damage. He looked at his watch and calculated her trip time. She had shaved off half her commute; the world was indeed fortunate.

He sipped his tea and wondered why she sat in the car. It must have been hot, and Kerri said she was upset. *Was he obligated to help her inside?* Maybe, but he didn't move from the window. He knew better than to offer help. She would resist because help was a weakness.

Roger shook his head. *Dear, dear Anita. You forever need to be in control.* It was the trait he hated the most.

Roger slipped out of sight while she gathered her things in the car. The windows shook as Anita entered the house and slammed the door. And Roger cringed as she announced her arrival. He huffed. *I know.*

"Roger? Where are you?" she yelled as she threw her day bag and purse on the table.

Roger stood in the dining room with his arms crossed. He was reluctant to face Anita and her mood. After a few breaths through his nose, he eased to the doorway and stopped. Anita's blouse clung to her back, and her arm glistened with sweat. Neither seemed to bother her. Instead, she dug around in her day bag and retrieved a wad of tissue.

"What's wrong?" he asked.

Anita whirled around at the sound of his voice. "I didn't hear you come in."

"I guess not." His tone was defensive as he moved into the kitchen. He grabbed the teakettle and filled it with water. "Do you want tea?" He turned on the burner but didn't face her.

She blew her nose and wiped the tears from her face. "You don't seem to be surprised that I'm here."

Roger cleared his throat before he spoke and assessed the situation. He guided her to a kitchen chair, brushed the hair off her face, and tucked it behind her ear. "No. I'm not surprised. And I am glad you made it home in one piece. I got a call from Kerri. She sounded concerned and told me you might come home. But she said you were upset and couldn't tell me why."

"Kerri had no right to do that! All she wants is to have my job, my discovery."

"Anita, she was just concerned." Roger shook his head. He didn't want to deal with this ongoing paranoid feud between Anita and her lab assistant. "After all these months, you still can't believe she is there to help you, not to steal your spotlight."

Anita huffed and crossed her arms. "You don't understand, Roger! She is the enemy."

"I understand perfectly well. And I won't go down this road again with you. Not today." He squatted in front of her and placed his hand on her knees. He looked deep into her eyes and searched for the intelligent Anita he loved. But all he saw was an upset child.

"What made you fly out of the lab?" Roger changed the subject so Anita would drop the 'Kerri' topic.

Anita opened her mouth, but the whistle from the kettle interrupted. Roger got up and filled the cups, then returned and sat in the chair beside her. He placed a hand on her knee and waited for her to explain.

"Go on, what's wrong?" he said.

Anita grabbed her oversized purse and retrieved a piece of paper. She shook it in front of Roger's face. "It's about this!" She shook the form as she rambled on. "I haven't felt well and didn't know why. I thought I had Typhoid Fever like you did when you returned from your trip."

Before he caught his tongue, he uttered, "Typhoid Fever! You're talking crazy."

"I'm not crazy!" Anita snapped.

Roger reared back into his chair and cleared his throat. "Anita,

I came down with that because of my trip to Uganda. I quarantined and treated before I came close to you. Plus, that was years ago."

Anita ignored Roger's statement. "So, I drew a blood sample. I did a complete panel of tests, thinking it was what you had the whole time. But this!" She shook the paper again.

He grabbed her arm to stop, and she released the tattered paper from her sweaty grip. Roger read it and reread it. Finally, he read it a third time, mouthing the words on the page, "Subject tests positive for Marburg Hemorrhagic Fever." Roger couldn't believe this had happened.

He looked up from the page and met Anita's gaze. Dazed, he could only muster, "I am so sorry."

Anita shivered. Roger grabbed a towel from the laundry room to wrap around her. "You should drink your tea. You need to keep your strength up." He stroked her cheek, and both were silent for a moment.

"What am I going to do?" Anita's voice was small and weak.

Roger's voice was solid and authoritative. "You're going to go upstairs, get out of these wet clothes, and get into a hot bath. While you are doing that, I will make you something to eat. Then we will figure this out."

Anita looked at him. "You sounded very stern just now. This isn't my fault." Then she softened her voice. "But I knew you would help me. You're right. I will go take a bath."

He matched her tone. "I know I sounded hard, but I am here to help. Now, go on, get upstairs."

Anita stood up, kissed Roger on the cheek, and shuffled out of the kitchen.

#

Roger dumped the tea and placed the cup in the sink. He needed something more potent and reached for a double old-fashioned glass, poured himself a vodka, and shot it back in one swig. The second shot was sipped as he leaned back against the kitchen sink. As the alcohol warmed his stomach, he waited to hear the water running before he let out a big, deep sigh of relief. *Was Anita's sickness a gift from God?*

He had lived in Charlotte for thirteen years and vicariously experienced Anita's journey on her quest for a Marburg virus cure. It had dominated her entire life, their lives. He and Anita both knew the progression of the virus. It would kill her within three weeks, four tops.

He hated Charlotte and couldn't wait to get out. But things had changed. This would all be over in another month, and he could start a new chapter in his life. The gift meant he didn't have to implement his exit plans. All he had to do was wait. Soon, he would be free of Anita's clingy grip, once and for all. The thought gave him a Cheshire Cat smile.

11: Roger

October 3, 2017

Anita bounded downstairs and pecked Roger's cheek as she breezed by on the way to the kitchen. "Good morning, Roger," she said in a sing-song voice.

"Good morning?" Roger questioned as he trailed behind her. "I researched herbal remedies last night and discovered that the Adler tree out in front is used as medicine. I went out before dawn and scraped for some bark to make tea. There is a cup waiting for you."

"Oh, Roger, you always take care of me. What's it supposed to do?"

"It soothes inflammation, fights infection, and supports liver function. And it is antimicrobial and an astringent."

"So?"

"We can use the leaves and bark to help with the rash." Roger pointed to the patch of redness that appeared on Anita's left cheek overnight. "It needs attention, or it will turn into lesions."

Anita touched her cheek but didn't respond to the comment.

Roger changed the subject. "I am surprised you are so chipper this morning and all dressed up."

"Now that I have been diagnosed with the Marburg virus, I

must change my focus. I'm thinking about myself and only myself right now. So, I decided I would wear the best outfit because I was worth it. Nothing is stopping me now."

Roger covered his mouth and coughed. *You sound like a deodorant commercial.*

Anita filled the teakettle and placed it on the stove. "I had a long talk with myself last night, and I came up with the framework of a plan. Everything is going to be alright."

Anita turned her back, and Roger was glad she didn't see his expression. He was speechless. *Delusions of grandeur.*

Anita continued her monolog, "Come, Roger, we need to talk. There're so many things I need to do." She waved him over to the table.

Roger hesitated before he eased into the chair. He fidgeted with his tie and cleared his throat. *What the hell is she going to say next?*

"Roger, there's no need to be nervous. Everything is going to be okay." She patted him on his knee.

The kettle whistled, and Anita popped up to remove it from the heat. Then, as Roger watched, she hurried around the kitchen, rearranged the countertops, and opened the cabinets to survey the contents.

"What are you doing?" Roger said, his voice packed with anxiety. This was his domain. "What are you looking for?"

"You know Roger, things in here don't make sense." She twirled around with her hands spread wide. "I want to cook you breakfast, and I can't find a thing," she said with an evil smile. "So, you know what we should do? Rearrange the cabinets! No, wait, we should get new cabinets. This place looks old and run down."

We are here together but on two completely different plains.

Roger wiggled in his chair and then got up and grabbed her arms to stop her movement. "Anita, calm down. You have only one thing you need to focus on right now. The cure is as important as it has always been, but now you are working against your time limit. Remodeling the kitchen will come later." He stared into her eyes, then he added softly, "If you find…when you find a cure and it makes you rich, you can remodel the whole damn house. Consider it a happy by-product for finding a cure."

Anita pouted as she rubbed Roger's cheeks. "Don't worry. I have a plan. Well, maybe not a complete plan thus far, but an idea to help me move along quicker." She wiggled out of his hold and continued to rifle through the cabinets and fridge.

I am talking a Tasmanian Devil off the edge.

He shook his head. "Come over here and drink the tea I made for you. I can fix breakfast. Then you can tell me all about your plan."

Anita stopped and faced Roger. She tilted her head like a curious dog. "Roger, even though I am sick, I am not crippled. I can still take care of myself. Mama was working right up to…."

Roger watched as a cloud of sorrow washed over Anita's face. Her shoulders slumped, and she slithered over the kitchen chair. It wasn't how Roger wanted to stop her frenzy, but he was glad she sat down.

He sat next to her and nudged the teacup towards her. "Drink this. It will make you feel better." It was nice to say, but he had no idea if it would help.

She sipped her tea, and when she finally spoke, all the bravo in her voice was gone. "I miss Mama. I miss both of them."

Roger reached over and stroked the clear cheek. "I know."

"Why did they have to die? Did Papa make Mama sick? Why did Mama kill him?" she asked.

Roger didn't have answers to any of these questions. All he knew was the person who asked wasn't a grown woman but the little girl who lost her parents violently at the tender age of 11.

Please don't let her life end the same way.

12: Roger

October 3, 2017

Roger waited patiently for darkness to fall over the neighborhood. Most people would be inside the little caves they called homes, and prying eyes would not see his actions. His dark-tanned skin helped at night when he didn't want to be noticed, physically and metaphorically. He zipped up the black tracksuit jacket and paced.

"Stop pacing. It makes me more nervous!" Anita snapped.

Roger stopped abruptly. He knew that as the night set in, so did disease-induced anxiety. Anita was in the first phase of the disease, but fuzzy thinking could take over at any time. He cursed himself for even knowing that bit of information. *Damn it. It wasn't his fight to fight!*

He wanted to head off the wild mood before it got nasty. The trick was to drug Anita before the full-blown attack peaked. The medication came from the alder tree that grew in the hedge between their house and the nosy neighbors.

They weren't really nosy, just active outside when they were home. Roger was glad the alder was in the front yard, not the backyard. The neighbors spent most of their time back there. Roger needed a little bark scraping, but the key was it had to be fresh, hence the tracksuit and the cover of darkness. *Everything had to remain a secret.*

Roger looked down at his outfit. He hated it. It made him feel like a ghetto thug. His preferred suits, dress shirts, and ties made him feel more successful, worthy, and accepted.

"Why the hell are you waiting? My skin is crawling, and you're just staring into space!" The words ejected out of her mouth like venom.

Roger paced again. The window of opportunity was about to close, and then the medication wouldn't alter Anita's mood. Would she become physically violent? Which was slower, the fall sunset or progressing dementia? He resumed his lookout post at the window.

Just a couple more minutes.

He turned away from the window and cautiously changed the subject. "I'll put some water on for the tea."

Anita opened her eyes and stared at him but said nothing; all she did was growl.

Roger felt the need to repeat. "I will put some water on, and it will be ready when I return with the alder bark." He patted her cheek on the way into the kitchen.

Roger filled the teakettle and placed it on the burner. While he waited, he reached for a double old-fashioned glass and poured himself a vodka. *If only Anita's tonic were as easily accessible as vodka.* The thought trailed off as the kettle sang.

"I think it is time now!" Anita shouted from the living room.

"Indeed, it is," he said aloud as he rinsed the glass and put it in the drying rack. He walked into the living room to pick up the bowl and switchblade placed next to the door on a side table. With one more glance outside, he opened the door and stepped out.

The air was cool and crisp, a pleasant change from the summer heat and humidity. Roger took a moment to drink in the sweet smells and the sound of crickets. These experiences were two things he never experienced before he came to Charlotte. Now, he didn't care if he ever experienced them again. He wanted out of this back-ass town. Roger had groomed himself for a bigger, better city than Charlotte, which was old, racist, and conservative. Soon, he would be free.

He looked down at his current outfit again. How had he gotten to the point in his life where he crept around in a tacky black tracksuit as he defaced the neighborhood trees?

Focus, Roger. He willed himself to walk over to the tree and complete his task.

He placed the bowl on the ground and groped the tree trunk to find a spot he could harvest without noticing it. If the neighbors discovered the damage, they might do something to "protect" the tree. He could see a fence around it and doused with fertilizer. That would render its bark useless. Worse yet, they could remove the alder, and the mammoth pecan is already scheduled to be removed. Roger and Anita had pushed for that tree to be removed for years, but now he wasn't sure he wanted it gone. They needed as much privacy as possible for the next month.

With patience and his back to the road, Roger found a patch of untouched bark. He bent down on his knees before the tree and scraped softly at the bark. The goal was to make the scraping as thin as possible, so Roger didn't have to waste time grinding it when he got back inside.

A car turned on the street, and headlights lit up the hedge as the car completed its turn. Roger ducked his head and froze like a garden statue while the flash of light washed over him. Overhead, he could hear the bats as they flapped away from their place behind the shutters.

Wouldn't that be a real shocker for the prim old ladies in the neighborhood? Roger hiding in the bushes? Roger chuckled. It reminded him of the first and only community meeting Anita, and he had gone to after buying the house.

13: Roger

May 2010 - Robbins Meadow Community Meeting, Charlotte, North Carolina

Anita and Roger had just moved into their house and received a flyer for the monthly community meeting. Roger thought this was an excellent opportunity to meet the neighbors. He heard good things about the neighborhood. The community prided itself on being a quiet place to raise a family. Not to say that was his goal, but still, it was a place where doctors and lawyers lived.

And it was a chance to portray the image he had practiced all his life. He wasn't a doctor or lawyer, but his new position as an Assistant Manager of Hospitality Services at Fairview University wasn't anything to disregard.

How quickly those dreams blew to hell.

Anita and Roger arrived at the community center well before the meeting. At the front door of the building, Anita opened it, and they were greeted with the chatter of conversation as it filtered out and surrounded them.

"Sounds like many people are already here." Anita stepped into the building, but Roger hesitated. Anita stepped back out. "Roger, what's wrong?"

"How do I look?" Roger grimaced the moment the question came out. He hated it when he showed his lack of confidence.

"Roger, you're being silly. You look handsome, as always."

Roger disregarded the comment because it didn't match her expression. She always brushed aside his concerns because she was a bull in a china shop. Roger preferred to slip in and survey the surroundings. But when they were together, Anita's way always won.

Roger made no attempts to move towards the door. Instead, Anita approached him and put her hands on his shoulders. "Roger, this is a great opportunity to meet new people, our neighbors. Look, more people are coming. Let's get in before they wonder why we are standing out here."

Roger didn't bother to look; he knew Anita was right. He took a deep breath and opened the door. Once inside, the door slammed shut behind him, and he involuntarily shuddered. *Stop being nervous.*

The entry hall was empty, but Roger could hear chatter in the distance. Anita patted him on the arm and took off towards the voices. He watched her turn the corner and disappear. Roger scrambled to catch up to her fast-paced stride. He rounded the corner and found Anita at the far end of the hall full of closed doors.

Once he reached her side, she said, "Here we go."

She opened the door, and they both moved into the meeting room and a sea of white-haired, overweight seniors. Every conversation stopped, and a hush settled over the room. Roger quickly took in the entire group as they stared at them. Anita and Roger were the only two youngish people in the room.

A woman with a bun of thick gray hair spoke first. "Are you looking for the Robbins Meadow Community Meeting?"

"Yes!" Anita said as she moved further into the room, apparently not distressed by the chill in the air.

On the other hand, Roger stood frozen at the door and made eye contact with those who had the gall not to look away. It was apparent to him that their arrival had shocked the group. It wasn't the first time and wouldn't be the last. He guessed the rumor mill had been hard at work, and they knew precisely who they were. He knew it would wear off, but he was tired of it.

Roger spotted a table with snacks and made a beeline for it, thankful for something to do with his hands and mouth. The general noise increased as he occupied his brain with the selection of sweets. Finally, he took a deep breath and let it out slowly.

We are over the first hurdle.

His moment of Zen was disrupted by the sound of a throat being cleared. "So, you are the new owners at the end of the block?"

Roger refocused on the two fat men and one woman on the other side of the table. "Yes, we moved in two weeks ago. My name is Roger. Nice to meet you." He extended his hand. Roger looked for any micro–expressions the fat man gave before he shook his hand.

"Welcome to the neighborhood. My name is Frank Visser, and this is my wife, Phyllis." He pointed to the lady who stood next to him.

Roger shook hands with her. "Nice to meet you, too." She exchanged a smile with Roger. "You have any accent. Where abouts do you hail from?"

"We are from Angola."

"Angola, you mean like in Africa?" Frank asked.

Roger jumped in and answered the unasked question, "I am Portuguese. Portugal ruled Angola until…."

Frank interrupted, "So you're Latino."

"No." Roger didn't want to explain the difference, so he changed the subject. "How long have you lived here?" He saw the cloud lift from Phyllis's face at the chance to let go of her husband's awkward comment.

"We have lived in this neighborhood since it was built," Frank said with pride.

Phyllis added her two cents. "There are quite a few of us who have." She motioned to the rest of the group.

Roger raised an eyebrow. *Was that a good thing or a bad thing?*

Frank continued. "It's a good thing you made it tonight. We'll discuss the criminal activity at your end of the street. It is on an uptick, you know. It happens every spring. People sneak around at night, "shopping" in our backyards and sheds." Frank put air quotes around the word shopping.

Roger blurted out. "I thought this was a nice neighborhood."

Phyllis was quick to respond. "Oh, it is. Don't let my husband scare you. It's just those people who walk up and down Route 4… going wherever they go…." She let her sentence trail off.

Tact was clearly not this couple's strong suit.

In the two weeks Roger and Anita lived in the neighborhood, he saw several people walking up and down the main road. It was only one house away. Roger agreed that the road, six lanes wide, was not a place to walk if you had the option to drive.

The disjointed conversation made Roger feel awkward, and it led to a slow burn in his belly. He took a sip of sweet tea and hoped that would settle his stomach. He shuffled from one foot to the other. What the hell was Frank going to say next?

"Well. Anyway, that is the main topic of tonight's meeting. We are making sure we keep our neighborhood safe and nice." Frank changed subjects. "So, Roger, who owns the hedge between your property and the neighbors?"

Roger furrowed his brow but didn't answer. *What an odd question to ask.*

Frank pushed on with his thoughts. "It looks…"

Phyllis piped in, "It looks trashy. Definitely not up to the standards WE have established for Robbins Meadow." She smiled.

Roger gave them a weak smile. "I believe it is the neighbors." His voice was not as strong as he would have liked. The hair on his neck bristled, and he could feel his face get warm. He placed his plate of sweets and drink on the table and clasped his hands in fists behind his back.

"Well, I will have to talk to them about that." Then, Frank turned and walked away.

Phyllis lingered and let her gaze shift around the room. "And don't get him going on the bat situation."

"Bats?"

"Why yes? Haven't you noticed the bats living in that enormous tree on the edge of your property? And I have seen them flying in and out from behind your shutters. You should have an exterminator come out and take care of them." Phyllis left to join her husband.

Roger was dumbfounded and outraged at the same time. His emotions made his blood boil, and he wanted to run. He looked for Anita to see if he could catch her eye, but her back was turned.

The community meeting was another opportunity to fit in. But the dream had evaporated with a few old, worn-out attitudes from the established elders. Yet again, he faced no acceptance, no matter how many degrees or prestigious job titles he and Anita had. Roger turned and stomped out of the room. Anita was close on his heels.

"What's wrong?"

"I was accosted at the snack table by the couple that apparently 'rule' over the neighborhood. He didn't seem to like me because I wasn't from around here." Roger threw his head back. He wished he hadn't said that. *You are just being oversensitive, Roger.*

"Really? You're kidding," she said.

Roger nodded. "They didn't come right out and say it, but he seemed pretty dismissive. His wife tried to smooth over his ignorance, but..."

"That's ridiculous. It's 2010, for God's sake. New South, my ass." Anita paced in front of Roger. Anita always paced when she was upset. He tried to be cautious of the open fire he had just stoked. He could see her eyes narrow while she decided what to do next.

She stopped her pace and stood in front of him. She held his shoulders and tried to look into his eyes. "Roger, you are better than they are. *We* are better." Roger turned his head from side to side to avoid her gaze. He always did when he didn't want to agree with Anita, his sister.

"Roger, are you listening to me? We will spend as much time here as we need. As soon as I get my doctorate, we will go back to Angola." She put her arms around him and squeezed him like when he was little.

The tender moment was interrupted by the woman with the bun. She poked her head out the door. "Wanted to tell you and your husband that the meeting is about to start." Then, before either Roger or Anita could correct her mistake, she was gone.

Anita refocused her attention from the door to Roger. "Fuck them." She stormed towards the room and left Roger in the hallway.

"No!" Roger charged the door and tried to grab Anita's arm.

She opened the door wide, rushed in, and ignored the group's stares. Then, with total disregard for what was in progress, she said, "I want to know one thing." She didn't wait for permission. Instead, she continued, "Does this neighborhood have any covenants?" The group wore confused expressions and didn't respond to Anita's question.

"Are you all deaf or dumb? Or both? Does this neighborhood

have any governing rules?" she snapped.

One of the board ladies spoke, "My name is Donna, and I am…."

Anita interrupted, "I don't care what your name is. Just answer my question!"

Donna said in a sweet but icy voice, "No, the neighborhood doesn't have covenants." She tried to extend a smile to Anita.

"Fine. I will live in my house and do whatever I damn well please, and you all can go to hell!"

Anita grabbed Roger by the arm and led him out of the building. "Asses. They don't know what they missed out on."

Behind the wheel of her BMW, she sat for a moment. "I wanted to fit in as much as you, Roger. But I will not let myself feel defeated. I am not the little girl I was in Angola or Germany. We have every right to be here as much as they do."

Roger leaned back against the headrest. *Another neighborhood and his sister was still his only ally. What the hell?*

#

Roger shuttered and brought himself back to the present. Did the memory bother him, or was it the thought of returning to Angola? Or maybe it was because his knees were wet from the dew.

He stood and brushed off the leaves from his tracksuit. He heard squeaks overhead and watched the bats fly from the colony behind the shutters into the tree next to the house.

Disgusting animals. They are the source of all our problems. At least the tree will be gone soon.

He huffed, picked up the bowl, and headed back inside. As he reached for the front door, he looked to see if anyone saw him and slipped inside.

Anita sat on her wing chair throne with her eyes closed. "Do you have it?"

"Yes, I've got it. Let me finish that tea." He hurried to the kitchen to make the tonic. He completed the task and brought back a mug to Anita. "Here you go. This should make you feel better."

Anita took the mug, tried to smile at Roger, and drank the tonic in one big gulp. Then she held the cup out for Roger to take and leaned her head against the wing.

Half-heartedly, she said, "Maybe we can try some honey in the tonic to make it taste better." Her eyes were closed, and her voice was gruff.

Roger responded, "We are trying to keep you away from sugar. Remember?"

She grunted in response, slowed her breath, and fell asleep.

Just like a bear going to sleep.

14: Bailey

October 4, 2017

Bailey had a hard day at work, but most days were. She was an office manager at a small start-up. The job was difficult, and it drained her. At home, a battle brewed with the neighbors about a tree. It was all too much.

The neighbors had gone all crazy and shit over that tree.

So, Bailey sat in her portable bubble and took a moment to regroup. She was reluctant to move and break the peace. The afternoon rainstorm finally showed up and beat the windshield. The thump of raindrops and the steamed windows reminded her of a thunderstorm during a trip to Arizona when the car's interior reached 103 degrees within minutes. It was so hot and sticky, just like the car right now. She felt like a steamed dumpling.

Typically, the couple went to the scheduled community meeting, if not for anything else, then to find out what the old biddies were up to next. But tonight, Bailey couldn't pull it together to be pleasant a moment longer. She was going to bail. She couldn't face the big old helping of bullshit from the Vissers, the Major, and his wife, about the maintenance of her hedge. And she sure as shit didn't want to talk about that damn tree.

Vissers and the hedge. The tree, those damn neighbors.

Both stressed her at the moment. The removal of the tree

would begin, and by the end of the week, it would be done. Maybe then the neighbors would leave them alone. Bailey smiled at the thought, and it gave her enough energy to get out of the car and head into the house.

Bailey opened the door. Jordan, her husband, and Alex, the dog, were there to greet her. "Hi, love," he said. "How was your day?"

She bent down to pat the terrier's head. "You know, same shit, different day." She saw the hurt in Jordan's eyes and added, "You know, same old, same old. How was your day?"

Jordan embraced Bailey. They were each other's rocks. Jordan held Bailey and said, "They'll be here by 8 a.m. tomorrow." Bailey didn't move; instead, she tightened her embrace, and her eyes welled up.

"I know it needs to come down because it's sick, but that we are doing it under duress pisses me off and makes me sad at the same time." She added as an afterthought, "I can't go to the meeting tonight." She didn't explain; Jordan would know why. "You don't have to go either. Why don't we just skip the meeting?" She waited for his response, but she already knew what it was. He wouldn't release himself from personal responsibility. He never did.

He rubbed her back. "I had a feeling you wouldn't go, but you know one of us has to represent. So, I'll sit through the meeting and cut out before socializing afterward."

Bailey gave him one more quick squeeze and dropped the embrace.

#

After Jordan left, Bailey soaked in the house's stillness. She enjoyed being alone when she was in a crappy mood. Her attitude made her not very nice to be around, which may be the point. Why did she always need to be around other people?

She sat in her office and tried to focus on writing, yet her mind wandered as it often did while she sat in this room. It was the room closest to the neighbors, and sometimes Bailey thought it had bad juju. Alex wouldn't come in and hang out with her while she worked. It only reinforced her theory. It was weird because the dog typically stayed close at hand.

Would Jordan think I was crazy or agree? She didn't know which.

A bang at the front door interrupted Bailey's daydream. Her back tensed.

Their house sat on the corner of Route 4, a multi-lane road at the entrance to a forgotten neighborhood. It was established during the building boom after WWII and billed as a country home for influential citizens to "beat the heat" of downtown. But that was then, and things had changed. The properties were still well kept, but the prominent citizens, the lawyers, and doctors, moved further out into more prominent and newer suburbs. The city grew up, and most forgot about the neighborhood. Now, the road that ran aside the community was also the approach of an on-ramp to a highway.

On average, cars would speed by at 45 or 50 miles per hour, but it also served as a well-beaten path for people who traveled by foot or bicycle. As a result, it wasn't unusual to find discarded bottles, food wrappers, or takeout food thrown onto the side yard that faced the road. Occasionally, they found people who sat or peed in the yard along the side of the road, but Alex ensured most didn't stay long.

Bailey worked by a small desk lamp in her office, and the lights in the living room were off, so the front of the house was dark. Bailey took advantage of the darkness and sneaked around the backside of the house to see who was banging on the door. She saw a dark figure through the gauzy curtain over the front door window. The rain stopped, but the wet road reflected the headlights and made it hard to see who stood on her doorstep.

The stranger banged again. Alex continued to bark as Bailey made out the figure of a short man. He looked down and away from the door.

Why won't he show his face?

Panic crept up in her throat, and her thoughts raced. She assured herself that Jordan had locked the back door and gate when he left.

Should she call the police? Technically, no, because whoever was on the doorstep hadn't done anything wrong. Yet. Should she call Jordan? His phone would be off during the meeting.

She moved around to the kitchen while Alex continued to bark. Right now, she had the advantage. She could see him, but he couldn't see her. But that would change if he made it inside. She would lose that advantage. She needed to protect herself so she could get out of the house and get help.

Bailey needed a weapon. *The knives.* She stood at the wooden knife block. Which one should she choose?

Her gut reaction was to go with the biggest knife. But she reconsidered that decision. She watched too many scary movies. She knew she might not control it, and it could be used against her if the blade got wet with blood. Or you sliced your own hand. *Go for the paring knife,* she advised herself. It was easy to conceal. You could make multiple quick stabs. If used against her, it wouldn't make wounds deep enough to cause death.

She grabbed the paring knife and headed to the front of the house. A second peek through the curtain showed nobody was there. Bailey ran up the stairs to the study, pulled at the blinds, and looked between two slats. She saw the back of a dark figure walked down the front path, onto the road, and back into the neighborhood. And then it dawned on Bailey; it was Roger, the next-door neighbor.

"Sure as shit, not going to open the door for that ass," she said as she turned from the window. Alex had stopped his noise and stood beside her in the dark study.

She patted his head. "Good boy, you chased the weird man away."

Roger creeped her out. Bailey couldn't figure out why he lurked around in the dark, and Anita was…well, she came off as rude and overbearing. Downright intimidating. She guessed Alex defensively acted out whenever he saw Roger or Anita because he read her nervousness around the neighbors.

The unexpected visit unnerved Bailey. She hoped Jordan would come home soon. Her concentration was gone. Instead, she held the paring knife close and spent the rest of the evening huddled in the dark.

15: Roger

October 4, 2017

Roger's head ached with anger. He stomped up the path to his front door. Anita sat in her wing chair and watched as he slammed the front door behind him. He unzipped the front of his tracksuit top, yanked it off, and threw it on the floor.

"I am so pissed," he growled.

"You look pissed. What did they say?" Anita's voice mirrored his anxiety.

"No one answered the door," he snapped back. "I know someone was home, and that damn dog kept barking and barking at the front door." Roger shook the paper in the general direction of the neighbor's house. The rage boiled up in Roger's body, and his face was hot and sweaty.

"Are you sick too?" she blurted out. "No, we have been meticulously clean around each other. Plus, you have the antibodies, so there shouldn't be any contamination." Her voice shook nervously. "My research had proven the disease had mutated. It is less contagious. So no, you couldn't be sick."

Are you trying to convince me or yourself? He stared but had tuned her out. At the moment, he didn't care what she said. He was distracted by his anger over the neighbors. *Maybe I should go and try again.*

"What?"

He could tell his foul mood had seeped into Anita's. He wished he had shown her the neighbor's estimate for the tree work after he made her tonic, but now it was too late. They had missed the window to take the nightly dose of alder bark, and now she would feel the effects.

"My stomach is upset. I'm freezing but sweating uncontrollably. My mouth is dry for one moment, and then I salivate the next," she whined.

Roger refocused. "I'll start the tea right away."

"I am going to need something stronger tonight. Can you fix me a drink?"

"What's your poison?" Roger said before he could catch his tongue. *Regrettable choice of words, Roger.* He didn't think alcohol was a good idea in her state, but it might knock her out.

Anita rested her head on the right wing of her chair. She turned just enough to look at him directly with one eye. She looked like a wild animal in her cave as she toyed with her captured prey before it became dinner.

Finally, she said, "I'll have what you are having." She closed her eyes.

Roger sighed. "Coming right up."

"Make it a double. With some water."

A moment later, he returned with two glasses filled to the rim. He handed one to Anita, "I propose a toast to the tree coming down, thus relieving us of the bat habitat and the insurance liability. Good riddance and fuck the neighbors. We won!" And with that, Roger drained his glass.

"Cheers." She sipped, then frowned. "This is very strong tonight. Did you put water in it?"

"Of course I did. It just seems strong because you haven't been drinking." *So, drink up and nighty night, dear sister.*

Roger wanted her asleep sooner than later before she went into a full-blown attack. However, the image of their mother's rage was still vivid in his mind.

16: Bailey

October 5, 2017

There was another bang on the door. The time was 6:30 a.m. Bailey looked through the front window and saw Roger. "Are you fucking kidding me?"

"Who's that banging?" Jordan stood atop the stairs with a towel wrapped around his clean but wet body.

Bailey rushed up the stairs. "It's fucking Roger! I can't deal."

Jordan rushed down the stairs and opened the front door. "What do you want?" he yelled through the locked storm door.

"I want to talk to you about this letter!" Roger said as he shook his fist.

"There's nothing to talk about. The work starts today."

"We will not pay for any of it!"

"Are you fucking kidding me? We have explained the situation several times. There is nothing more to say."

"Come out here and tell me what the process will be," Roger demanded.

"I'm in a towel! No, I am not coming out. You went back on your word to pay for half of the tree removal, which means you have no right to know anything more." Jordan slammed the door and watched Roger leave.

Bailey sat on the stairs and cried. "It isn't going to end, is it?"

Jordan said nothing. He didn't have to. They both knew the answer. Jordan moved by Bailey and headed back upstairs. Bailey followed behind and entered the study to watch Roger leave their property. *But this isn't over or the end.*

Professor Belo's journal entry:

Journal Entry: October 5, 2017

Scope– Monitoring of the progress of Marburg Hemorrhagic Fever

Identification–Patient Alpha 1 (A. Belo)

Appraisal–

Physical attributes–Overall not feeling well / fever, headache, chills, and muscle pain. Addition of rash, abdominal pain, nausea, vomiting, and diarrhea.

New behaviors– Fatigue, irritability, and confusion.

Patient Alpha 1 notes–Skin feels like bugs are crawling under the surface.

Analysis–Patient Alpha 1's symptoms aligned with the first stage and swiftly progressed into the late phase of the first stage, the early organ failure phase of the Marburg Hemorrhagic Fever.

Report–Day 4 of the virus: despite the current symptoms, the patient remains in good spirits.

17: Anita

October 5, 2017

Anita's belly burned as she stood at the living room window and spied on the tree removal men setting up their equipment. A ping of pain jabbed at her stomach, and she debated whether it was a physical symptom of the Marburg Virus or an emotional reaction to her anger about the tree next door.

She had never come up against anyone as stubborn as the neighbors. Anita couldn't control the situation, and every time she thought about it, it made her furious. They were gnats and needed to be squashed. How dare they defy her, but they were! She hoped the tree would be gone within a few hours and the threat of property damage would disappear. Anita let an evil smile form on her lips when she realized she had gotten her way after all.

She shook her head. The silly neighbors tried to use reason and logic with Roger and Anita. Anita didn't want to hear it. And she didn't want to see that damn survey they used as evidence. Roger should never have offered to pay for half of the removal in the first place. But then they decided they didn't have to pay for half because of the survey. They were responsible if the tree was entirely on the neighbor's property.

That had gone over well. Not.

Another ping in her stomach brought her back to the present.

She moved from the window and went to the kitchen, where she intended to work. Unfortunately, the work crew was at the base of the tree, and even though the windows were closed, and the air conditioner hummed, she could still hear the chatter. They were right outside the laundry room, connected to the kitchen.

She sat down, tried to concentrate on her work, and ignored the noise. But she was distracted by the conversations and the waves of pain in her stomach. She gave up and entered the laundry room to eavesdrop on their conversations instead of her research.

Curiosity killed the cat. So, what?

Anita peeked through the blinds to put faces to voices. The tree removal crew consisted of three men. The first man was older, taller, and skinnier than the others and wore rock climbing gear. His assistant was younger and shorter. The third man was fat and red-faced.

The skinny one said, "That's an extremely tall tree. And look, I have no room to move around here! No wonder why we couldn't use the cherry picker." He pointed to the hedge on either side of the tree trunk.

The red-faced man huffed as he trailed behind the first workman. "Keep in mind, the next-door neighbors don't want us on their property."

The skinny one stopped mid-stride and turned around to face his supervisor. "You're fucking kidding me! And we aren't using the cherry picker."

"No. You'll have to do it all by climbing the tree and taking it down piece by piece."

Lanky threw up his arms. "It's a fucking 75-year-old tree, and it has a rotten middle! How far down does the rot go?"

"I don't know. Just be careful," the supervisor said as he lit a cigarette.

Lanky got up close to the supervisor, "Be careful? I have been climbing trees for thirty-plus years...."

"Listen, do what you need to do and for as long as it takes. The owners have agreed it's more important to be slow and safe, even if that means they pay more. So, let's get this job going." The supervisor walked back to the truck.

Anita couldn't contain her satisfaction. She and Roger had successfully made the neighbors pay extra for the tree service, which served them right for the hard time they gave Roger and her about it. So yes, she had gotten her way in the end.

Her happiness gave her the energy to pack up her work and go to the office. She couldn't work here with all the noise.

Professor Belo's journal entry:

Journal Entry: October 6, 2017

Scope– Monitoring of the progress of Marburg Hemorrhagic Fever

Identification–Patient Alpha 1

Appraisal–

Physical attributes–Fever, headache, chills, muscle pain, rash, abdominal pain, nausea, vomiting, and diarrhea—additionally, Conjunctivitis, swelling of legs and feet, and blood evident in stool and vomit.

New behaviors– Labored breathing.

Patient Alpha 1 notes–Why is the disease progressing at an accelerated rate?

Analysis–Patient Alpha 1 has moved entirely into the late phase of the first stage, the early organ failure phase of the Marburg Hemorrhagic Fever.

Report–Day 5 of the virus, anxious of death.

18: Anita

October 6, 2017

Less than a week, and Anita could sense the disease as it took over her body. The symptoms moved quickly into the late phase of the first stage. She was surprised that the confusion, aggression, and dementia expected in the second had already seeped in.

During the day, she could hold it together, but the details of reality faded away late at night. At night, the actual truth and "what ifs" commingled. After dinner, she withdrew to her bedroom like a bear who retreated for winter hibernation.

Her bedroom was her safe cave and reflected her home from the past. She painted the walls and ceiling in a deep midnight blue matte paint that reminded her of Angola's night skies. The floor was covered with a thick but rough clay-colored carpet that mimicked sand and dirt. The furniture was sparse in the room. Her bed was in the center of the room, a four-drawer dresser, and a writing desk with a chair.

The dark mahogany furniture had patches of lighter-rubbed wear. Anita saw no reason to spend money on them because no one saw them. After all, the wornness reminded her of her childhood home. And none of it would come with her when she left this place.

A wicked thought crossed her mind. Maybe she should light a

match and walk away from the whole house. She giggled out loud at that thought. But as quickly as she laughed, her mood darkened, and her smile melted. Setting the village on fire was precisely what the military had done after the disease devastated the natives. A sour expression crossed her face. The military felt it was the only way to eliminate the evil that had settled in the village. Stupid people didn't realize they'd spread the disease wider.

Anita sat on the bed's edge and looked around the room. Tonight, the scene was different. It wasn't just a bookcase full of journals and her only childhood doll. It was a representation of her whole life. She contemplated that thought for a moment and decided it was pretty miserable. *Had she done all this work for nothing? Did anyone care if she found the cure?* She knew the university didn't care and didn't think Roger did either.

She walked to the bookcase, picked up the doll and a journal, and sat at the desk. She stroked the doll's yarn hair and hummed the song her mother hummed when she braided Anita's hair. Then, she opened the journal and reread the history. She felt there was something that she hadn't seen yet. Maybe tonight, she would find the answer.

In the spring of 1967, an order was placed for 18 primates to be delivered to Marburg, Germany, for use in a polio research lab. The farm workers started their usual routine of beefing up the monkeys before shipment.

The day before the shipment shipped out, they gathered the monkeys, who responded well to the added food, and realized they were short three for the order. Their solution was to look for three more from a remote farm area where they had separated monkeys that were too skinny. They picked three that could pass for healthy and included them in the shipment. The monkeys were delayed in London for quarantine before being released to the German government.

In reality, the first German-bound monkey to display signs of disease had exhibited signs before it left Uganda. However, neither the handlers nor the research lab employees noticed or understood the early progression of Hemor-

rhagic Fever.

Six monkeys died within two days of arriving at the lab. They stopped the research for a week to see if the others would become sick. Once there were no signs of the fever, the study resumed. The remaining twelve monkeys were used to further the research until they became ill. In the end, all 18 monkeys were dead. Thirty-one employees were sick, and seven died of the disease known now as the Marburg Virus, commonly called Bat Crap Fever.

At the time, no one knew how the virus spread. And the fever track from monkey to human was part of the mystery. The link between the two was not present at first. The human and the monkey exhibited different symptoms at every stage of the disease. Further investigation determined the monkeys had carried the disease from Uganda, though some speculated that the fever originated in London during the delay. Besides the 1967 Germany outbreak, the virus was recorded only in Africa. It was concluded that the monkeys native to the region were the carriers.

But where did the monkeys get the disease? Again, the evidence led back to the living conditions on the farm. This led to the mango fruit being un-harvested and the main staple for the monkeys and other animals, including fruit bats.

Fruit bats were known to be the carriers of the fever, hence the common name of the disease. Though they are carriers, they seldom contract the disease, which makes it challenging to track down and contain the infected animals. The bats ate the fruit by squeezing the juice out of the flesh, leaving the skin and flesh covered in contaminated bat spit and bat crap. Then, the monkeys and other animals eat the leftover fruit and contract the deadly, incurable disease.

Anita peeled back the sticky note from the page and held it at eye level to read in her handwriting. *Current studies still show that the mortality rate among animals is 100%, and 90% is for humans.*

Anita taped the note back on the page and closed the journal. She placed the doll down and blew her nose. Even though she knew this history by heart, she still choked up. It was clinical from an outsider's point of view, but it was her history. For Anita, this was her story retold.

90% mortality rate for humans.

It was unacceptable. Now more than ever, she needed to speed up the pace of her experiments. Standards and procedures that the university demanded in the research wouldn't do anymore. She needed to go from calculated processes that took weeks or months to a day or two. She needed answers fast.

She needed a new vehicle and a way to administer the virus. Lab rats and syringes wouldn't do anymore. They were too slow and cumbersome. She needed something more significant. *Could she get something like a monkey?* She chuckled at the thought that the one animal that started the whole thing would be the same animal that saved the world.

How about people?

Anita heard a voice, then swiveled in her chair to see if someone was in the room. Who said that? Did she say that, or was it all in her head? She looked around again, but she was alone.

How about people? *Anita, you have all of those undergrads in your classes.* Some of them might be eager to be a part of the research. Anita bet some wouldn't even be missed if they happened to get sick and die. *So, what do you have to lose?*

"My own life," Anita said out loud.

She turned off the desk lamp and picked up her only toy from childhood, the doll she took with her when she fled Angola. She nuzzled it and then sneezed from the collected dust in its hair. Even though the doll was dirty from decades of wear and tear, she refused to wash it. It was her only connection to her homeland.

Anita crawled into bed and stared at the ceiling, stroking the doll's hair. Could she really do what she was thinking? The more she thought about the idea, the more her mind resolved it was the right thing to do. *For the greater good.*

What was it Joseph Stalin said? "You can't make an omelet

without breaking a few eggs."

19: Roger

October 7, 2017

"Roger, are you listening to me?" Anita stopped searching through the kitchen cabinets and snaked her arms around Roger's midsection from behind. She held him close with her mouth near his ear. "Roger, you're daydreaming. Where did you go?"

Roger didn't answer her. Instead, he broke her grip, took a few steps forward, and stared out the window over the sink. Anita didn't know he had created an exit plan and that she wasn't playing her part correctly. It made him a little crazy.

"It isn't going as planned," he muttered.

"What's not going as planned? I don't even have a plan. What are you talking about?"

"What? No. Nothing." He turned to face Anita, who sat at the kitchen table and ate dry cereal from the box. "You need to eat that with milk."

"You sounded like Papa just now. I don't like it." She pouted but then lifted her head and gave Roger a big smile.

Roger wasn't sure how to interpret the mood swing Anita had just displayed. It reminded him of how his mother was once she had "The Fever." He shook that image out of his head and changed the subject.

"Tell me why you are in a good mood today." He brought her a bowl, a spoon, and a quart of milk. Then he poured the cereal into the bowl with milk and placed it in front of Anita.

Roger watched as she took two big spoonfuls and spoke. Milk sprayed his face. He wiped it off. *I could smack you right now.*

He took a deep breath. "Just because you are sick doesn't mean you can stop being civilized. Chew and swallow your food, and then speak." Again, he channeled Papa's mood, although Papa would have commanded instead of requested.

Anita looked at him and finally placed her spoon down, "You are right. I went upstairs last night in quite an awful mood. I was scared and confused. I wanted to bury my head and hope it wasn't true. But I knew I couldn't. So, I sat down and reread my journal from the early days of my research. While I read the background history of the virus, a question popped into my head." Anita made sure she had Roger's attention.

"Why not use humans for the experiments?" Anita flew her hands up like she'd done a magic trick.

Roger sat there dumbfounded, and his head filled with a multitude of questions. How crazy was she? *How long did she have the disease before she became symptomatic? Did he need to lock his bedroom door before going to bed? Was the end closer than he had planned?*

"Roger? Did you hear me?" Anita poked him in his arm.

"Yes, I heard you. Are you crazy?" As the words slipped out of his mouth, he regretted it.

"Don't use that word around me! You know that isn't nice!"

"I am sorry. I'm sorry. It was insensitive. Tell me, what are you talking about?" He held his breath. He hoped she was kidding. Doubtful, *Anita isn't a funny person.*

"Reading my notes last night, I returned to the same problem. The lab rats didn't progress through the known course of symptoms to the second stage because they didn't live long enough. There just isn't enough time for the vaccines to take effect. But as I reread my notes, I thought maybe they didn't show all the symptoms because they are rats." Anita took a moment to eat a couple of spoonfuls of cereal.

Where was she going with this? Panic built up in his stomach. *Stop stalling.* He was impatient and prompted her, "The rats didn't get sick because they are rats?"

Anita slapped his hand. "Yes! Exactly, the rats didn't get sick because they are rodents."

Roger looked confused.

"The Marburg and Ebola viruses live in the digestive systems of fruit bats. So even though bats aren't rodents, maybe rats have the same immunity to the virus." Anita stated as if the discovery was so elementary, everyone should get it.

"Okay…, so you are saying the lab rats were immune to the virus because they already had it?"

"Well, yes, in a way. What I am saying is that lab rats naturally have antibodies. Meaning. They were not the best animals to experiment on in the first place."

He could see the relief on Anita's face, but Roger didn't follow her thought process. He impatiently waved his hand. "So?"

"I need to find a different animal to do experiments on, and then it just popped into my head. Why not humans?" She brought the bowl up to her lips and drank the milk. When she was done, she wiped her mouth with her palm. "So, what do you think?"

Roger sat back in his chair. His knee-jerk reaction was to get as far away as possible from her. But then, in a flash, he recalled when the doctor told their father to send their mother away and let her die in peace. The thought intensified the panic in his stomach. He got up and moved to the other side of the room.

"Anita, I think we need to look at what you are proposing more closely." Roger paced back and forth. So many emotions flooded him, and he wasn't sure which he should express.

"Roger, calm down. It is all in the name of science. It's okay. We really won't be hurting anyone." Anita forced herself not to smile. "You know, when we leave here, it would be great to have a world-renowned scientist give you a job recommendation."

"You are my sister. The world knows you as my wife. Seriously. Everyone would think it was a biased recommendation. And stop changing the subject!" *And stop trying to control me!*

"Not everyone knows us as husband and wife, just the dopes in this neighborhood. Who cares what they think? We've been here for ten years, and they have been nothing but rude to us." Her eyes clouded, and she trailed off momentarily before returning to the primary subject. "I want to recruit humans for my studies." Anita stayed silent while she waited for his response.

"You don't want to hurt them, do you?" He knew he sounded like a scared little boy's request. *How much damage could Anita do in the limited time she had?*

She interrupted his thought. "Think of it as a game. Like we are in Vegas, picture it. We're both dressed to the nines and gliding through the casinos. People stopping and staring because we look and feel fabulous." She got up and went to Roger. She got close to his ear and placed her hand on his arm. "We won't hurt anyone. Come play with me in Vegas."

20: Roger

October 8, 2017

Alone and in broad daylight, Roger shivered at the plan they had agreed to carry out. It centered on a way to infect her study group's students without their consent. After hours of discussion, Anita dismissed the idea of having them volunteer willingly because she didn't have that much time.

Roger tossed out a snarky suggestion of candy laced with arsenic, and Anita jumped on the concept. It was an idea he regretted. It was too familiar, and traces of the poison would be discoverable. But Anita was hell-bent on the plan, so Roger folded like a house of cards.

Anything to move him closer to his goal.

Luckily, Anita often offered snacks to all her study groups throughout the semester, so it wasn't new. What was different was how Roger had to hide the virus. The trick was to have a flavor that would overpower or mask the taste. Typically, he made sweet snacks, cookies, bars, and cake for Anita's meetings. His head filled with so many questions.

Was sweet the correct disguise? Would sweet, bitter, or sour work better? Perhaps, but would offering something different throw up red flags? How clued in were these students? Did the virus have a taste? Did it have a smell? You couldn't just sprinkle the virus on top of some cookies like powdered sugar, could you?

He had lots of questions and little time to investigate. Roger sat down at the kitchen table with a stack of cookbooks. As he browsed, his mind wandered back to Angola and what his mother used to make for them as a treat. They rarely had sugar, but it usually came as Portuguese Burnt Sugar Candy.

"God, that was sweet," Roger said out loud.

That was it. It would be the perfect vehicle for the virus. So sweet and irresistible. Roger dug through the pile of old cookbooks of Portuguese favorites and found the recipe. He wrote a list of ingredients and headed out to the store.

Roger returned with his supplies and made the candy. He loved this part. He loved his time in the kitchen when he dove into experimentation. It gave him purpose and always made Anita happy. Anything and everything to make her happy.

But the big question gnawed at Roger's brain while he worked. *Could Anita hurt or even kill unsuspecting people? Was this a crazy idea concocted by someone who had lost her mind or a leap of faith from a brilliant scientist? Are they the same?*

Roger still had faith that she could indeed find a cure. He loved his sister, but she needed his help to get her to the finish line. The sooner she got there, the sooner he would be free himself. The crushing noise on the gravel drive broke his concentration.

She came in like a rush of foul air, just like she always did. "What smells so divine?" She threw her bag on the table and hugged Roger from behind.

Roger stiffened. He hated it when she manhandled him. "I am working on some Burnt Sugar Candy. Do you remember it from when we were kids?"

"Oh, my God! Of course I do! Is it ready? I want some."

"No. It isn't ready. But you'll be the first to get it when it is."

Roger was pleased that the candy lightened her mood.

Anita squealed, "Roger, I am so glad we're on the same page!"

"You bring baked goods to the study group meetings anyway, so why not feed them food laced with the virus?" Roger said as he stirred the liquid candy. "I figured the candy was sweet enough to hide any off taste the virus might have. By the way, does the virus have any taste or smell?"

Anita was silent while she thought about the question. "I don't know. It's never been an issue I needed to worry about in my clinical studies."

"I figured that might be the case, so I went with something so sweet it would not be noticed if there was. And because no one has had the candy before, they wouldn't know if the taste was off."

"Oh, Roger, I am glad you came up with this idea. It warms my heart that you are so helpful, and it frees my mind to find a cure."

Roger came over and put his hand on Anita's cheek. "I would do anything for you, my dear sister." Anita leaned into his touch and then turned to kiss his hand.

"Could you make me tea and bring it to my room?"

"Are you not hungry?"

"No, my stomach is in pain, and I want to get some rest. Is the candy going to be ready for my study group tomorrow?"

"If all goes as planned, yes, it will be."

21: Anita

October 9, 2017

Anita bounded down the stairs and into the kitchen. "Good morning, Roger! What a great day it is!"

Roger was sitting in the corner, sipping tea. "There's hot water in the kettle and. . . ."

"Is there any candy for me?" Anita eyed the box on the table. "Can I have a piece?" She reached for the container.

Roger smacked her hand away. "No. Don't touch them. They are not for you, if you know what I mean."

"Roger, you said I would be first to taste. But you didn't save any for me?"

"Yes, I did. But before I let you taste, we must discuss how to present this to your group."

"What do you mean?"

"You can't plop the box down and say eat up without partaking too, right?"

"I guess so."

"I need you to look at this box. Hold the box with the lettering facing you, then open it, and take the piece of candy from the right-hand corner closest to you before setting it on the table."

"We don't have a table," she said shortly.

The randomness broke Roger's thoughts. "What?"

"We don't sit at a table. We sit at desks with those arm thingies in a circle."

Roger shook his head. "Okay. I need you to take the piece from the right-hand corner closest to you before you hand it to the next person."

"Why that corner?"

Roger cracked his neck to release his tension. "Because it's the only one that isn't treated." He stared at her.

Anita let the answer roll around in her head before she finally understood. "Oh, Roger. That is so clever. I am so lucky to have you."

#

Controlled excitement was hard for Anita when she stepped into the classroom they used for the study group. She had to tell herself repeatedly to stay in control and be serious. She took deep breaths to settle herself as she prepared the room for the group.

You're trying too hard to make a good impression. The students will see right through that. Anita forced herself to sit down. She stared at the empty chairs; soon, they would be filled with new participants for her studies. It didn't matter who they were as long as she got what she wanted, what she needed.

In the quiet, she allowed herself to relax and to let the "in control" persona slip. She found it harder to live the two separate lives she was sentenced to each day. Both competed for her attention like little children. Neither got her full attention or energy, and both suffered. It drained her, and she wasn't sure how long she could keep up the charade. One of her lives would win, and she wasn't naïve enough to believe it would be the healthy one. No, she knew all too well the virus would take over soon. Her mind jumped back to the present. *Where were the students? Shouldn't they be here by now?*

The door answered her question as it banged open, and ten people rushed in. Anita gave a slight smile. *Come, sit. Would you like a piece of candy, little boy?*

"Hey, sorry we are late. The elevator got stuck," a tall young man said. She noticed the exchanged looks among the ten as they sat in a circle.

"Trapping all ten of you? That's convenient." Anita said. *Asses, you all deserve to get sick—You're all useless. You wouldn't even be here if you were better students. I am doing a good thing, thinning the herd of low performers.*

She walked to the door and closed it. "Well, you are here now. Where did we leave off last time?" She walked about the group, staring at them with death rays before taking her seat.

"Oh, before I forget." She dug into her bag. "My husband made this candy for us. It's one of my favorites." Anita made sure the writing was facing her, plucked the corner candy, and popped it in her mouth. She passed the box to her left and watched as each student took a piece and ate it.

Let the games begin.

22: Anita

October 11, 2017

Anita sat at her desk and waited for the first student to visit during office hours. It had only been two days since she started her experiment with her students, but she hoped signs of the disease would be present.

In its purest form, the Marburg virus had an incubation time of two to 21 days before the onset of symptoms. The progression of the disease was two weeks before it ended in death. Anita believed she had a mutated strain and a longer timeline. She also theorized the antibodies that had protected her throughout her life made the disease linger in her system. The virus wouldn't be so kind to the students. *At least they won't suffer as long as she has.*

She was at the point where she threw caution to the wind. Anita spent her time in the lab concocting as many varieties of vaccines as she could. Anita had Kerri work on a more controlled and traditional course of experiments. Anita suspected it was useless, but why not open all her options?

Kerri.

Anita still wasn't sure of her intent. She was paranoid that Kerri was a spy for a German research team currently working on the same cure. It was too convenient that Kerri appeared just before the denial of her extension. Was she a spy for the university? They couldn't. Why would they knowingly hire someone to steal her funding? The simple answer was that they wouldn't. But Anita still didn't trust Kerri. Once she found the cure, she would fire Kerri. *Or maybe she could become a lab rat herself...*

A knock on the door interrupted Anita's mental rant. *It is time to put on the concerned professor's face.* She smoothed her hair and folded her hands on her desk. "Come in."

"Hi. Thanks for seeing me. I wanted to talk to you about your class," the young lady said as she slid into the guest chair across from Anita.

Anita noted her general appearance. The student's skin appeared to be waxy and had lost color. Her eyes were sunken and rimmed with red.

The student wrapped her sweater tight around her midsection and looked around the room. "Is it cold in here?"

"Maybe. I tend to keep it on the cool side. It helps me focus."

"Really? I find the complete opposite. I can't seem to get warm or stay focused. That's why I wanted to meet with you. Is there any way to take a leave of absence?"

"No!" Anita answered abruptly.

"What?"

Anita saw the shock in the student's eyes and tried to backpedal. "You're too close to the end of the semester. It isn't possible. Tell me, what is going on?" Anita leaned in to hear all the details.

"I think I have the flu. My stomach is really upset."

"Really? The flu? Why would you think that? Would you like some Tums?" Anita ignored the student's discomfort. She was too focused on the data she needed. So instead, she grabbed one of the five bottles of Tums from the desk drawer, labeled "1." She shook as she placed it on the desk between them. "Tell me how you are feeling."

The student's eyes began to tear up, and Anita's patience wore thin. It took a lot of effort to show empathy and compassion. She pushed the Tums closer to the edge of the desk. "Go on. It will make you feel better." The pills in her desk had been treated with a version of a cure.

The student hesitated before she took the bottle and opened up the lid. She shook out three tablets and popped them in her mouth. As she chewed, her face contorted before she swallowed hard.

"Those were a little chalky." She dug a water bottle out of her bag to wash the antacid down.

Anita noted on her notepad the student's name, current condition, and which antidote formula she had taken. "If there's nothing else, you are free to go." Her tone was accented with a wave of the hand. *I have too many rats to see.*

The student looked confused. "But..."

Anita got up and opened her office door. "Thanks for coming to see me. Keep me posted on how you feel tomorrow." She ushered the student out and shut the door behind her. Anita let a satisfied grin cross her face. The virus was already showing the first stage of illness. *This may be easier than she thought.*

#

By Wednesday, Anita saw six of the ten students from her study group. Her curiosity burned about those two. Did they feel sick? Did they have antibodies as she did? She needed answers, but she couldn't seek them out. If she showed any concern for them, it would seem odd. They needed to come to her freely.

"Why don't you have them here for a study group?" Roger suggested.

"What?" Anita snapped back to the present. Nowadays, she spent more time lost in her thoughts and quickly forgot that Roger was around.

"Have the study group here, and then we both can observe them."

"What about the neighbors?" Annoyed that they had any say in her private life.

"What about them?" Roger said.

"We never have people over."

"Well, it's really none of their business."

"I agree. But there will be so many cars. We have made such a big deal about their visitors' parking in front of our house. They will notice us having a house full of guests."

Roger threw his book against the wall. "I don't give a shit about the neighbors! We can have as many people as we want over here. They can't say a damn thing."

"Roger, calm down. As I was saying, the last thing we want is for people to pay attention to us. You are right. It is none of their business, but still. We have to be very careful."

23: Roger

October 12, 2017

The study group meeting was like a drug-induced orgy out of the 1960s. Roger shook his head to clear it, but the motion only made him nauseous. He shouldn't have drunk so much. Time and space slipped through his fingers last night. He didn't look forward to the scene of destruction created last night. It made him uncomfortable, as these people had invaded his personal space. They touched his things. But, as mad as the situation made him, it gave Anita the data she needed. Roger was surprised at the range of degradation among the group members, from sicker than Anita to no signs of the virus.

Anita insisted that the group carpool so as not to raise suspicions among the neighbors. Roger could tell the students resented the idea, but they all complied. Roger wondered if it was because they were too sick to argue or were usually submissive. Either way, it didn't matter.

Roger could smell the remnants of last night's party before he made it completely downstairs. *How long would it take to clean the mess?* At least he didn't have Anita around to help him. She wasn't good at domestic tasks. Since she got sick, she made more of a mess than helped.

Roger stopped at the landing to look out the small window.

He could see one of the student's cars still parked outside. *Was that there when he went to bed?* Anita and a couple of the students lingered at the night's end when Roger went to bed. *Had they fallen asleep here?* Roger shuddered. The last thing he wanted to do was to deal with sick, hungover people!

He strolled through the living room and picked up wine glasses and food wrappers as he went. Disgust fueled his foul mood. *How much longer would he have to deal with this drama?*

Roger stopped at the doorway to the dining room. One student slumped at the table face first. Damn it! He placed the glasses down and shook his shoulder. There was no response. He shook harder, and the body leaned towards Roger. He took a step back as the body fell out of the chair onto the floor at Roger's feet. His hand flew up to his mouth to hold the vomit as he ran to the kitchen sink. In his rush, he didn't see the second body propped up in the laundry room doorway.

No, no, no, what has she done? He spat out the foul taste in his mouth and rinsed it with water. He turned away from the sink after a few deep breaths. He knew he had to check if the person was alive. But he already knew he wasn't. So, did they die naturally, or had Anita done something to force the death? It didn't matter. He was screwed either way.

Roger went to the dining room and knelt next to the body. He eased it to be face up and felt for a pulse. The body was already stiff. It was dead.

He fell back onto his butt and rocked back and forth as he hugged his knees tight.

It can't be. It wasn't supposed to happen like this; no one was supposed to get hurt.

Roger's thoughts raced back to the night their parents died. Had the disease turned Anita into a copy of their mother?

As Anita got sicker, he hadn't allowed himself to think of what could happen. He'd always assumed she would pull through. But now, faced with a dead body, he realized she would only worsen. Either way, Anita and Roger were now murderers.

He couldn't help himself. He cried. As the tears ran down his cheeks, he chastised himself. Tears were for little boys. His body shook. *Damn you, Anita!*

All he ever wanted was to be on his own and live his life without her. But now, they were tied together for the rest of his life. She would die, but he would be stuck with the consequences.

"Roger? What's going on?" Anita appeared in the doorway of the dining room.

Roger mumbled to himself. "Go away, just go away."

"Roger? What happened to Steve?"

Roger jumped up and rushed to Anita. He got up close to her face and yelled, "Is that his name?"

"What did you do to him?"

"What did *I do* to him? Funny Anita! He was alive when I went to bed. Now he is dead! What did you do to him?" Roger poked at Anita's chest.

Anita pushed by him and checked the body for a pulse.

"I already did that!" Roger said.

Roger towered over her as she turned to meet his eyes. "You don't have to be so mean."

"Mean!" Roger flapped his arms in excitement. "We have a dead body in the middle of our dining room. You said you wouldn't hurt anyone, and I believed you. How stupid I was, and now I'm an accomplice to murder!" Roger huffed and flapped his arms again. "I think I can speak any way I want!"

"Shush. It isn't murder. He obviously died from the virus."

"Are you sure?"

"Well, not completely."

Roger paced, "Oh, my God! What did you do last night after I went to bed? Did you help him along to the great beyond?"

"Roger, calm down. You are talking crazy." Anita slid into one of the dining chairs.

"Crazy! What's crazy is that you are so calm!"

"Roger, stop it!"

Roger rubbed his face as he paced. "Once there is an autopsy, they'll figure out what is happening! We are going to go to jail!"

"Roger! There isn't going to be an autopsy."

Roger stopped in his tracks and stared wide-eyed at Anita. "What?"

"There isn't going to be an autopsy because there isn't going to be a body." She brushed a piece of lint off her shirt.

"No, no, no. What are you thinking?"

"We will get rid of the body in the backyard."

"What?!" Roger shook his head vigorously.

Anita stood up and came close to Roger's face. "It's perfect. Even though the neighbors took that tree down, no one can see our backyard from any direction."

"Oh God, you have already thought this through." Roger covered his face with his hands.

"Well, yes. I needed to plan out every aspect of my research. That included disposing of failed experiments."

"We can't just throw them away like lab rats!"

"No, we incinerate them."

"The bodies?"

"No, the rats. Roger, listen very carefully to me. We will dissolve the bodies and then bury the remains in the backyard."

Roger was stunned. *Dissolve the bodies. How? Did she really think he would agree to this? Did she really think this was going to work?*

Roger looked at her and searched for some sense of clarity and sanity. All he saw was a woman who had once been beautiful, now covered in open sores. They looked like infected zits that pocked her tan skin. Roger looked away. Afraid her conjunctivitis would burn a hole in his brain.

"Roger. Don't even think about calling the cops. If I go to jail, the research will stop. That is a death sentence for me. Do you want me to die?" Her voice was small, and she sounded scared.

Roger didn't answer. *Yes, he did. Why wasn't she dead already?*

Anita shifted to an authoritative voice. "If you don't go along with the plan, you are no good to me."

"What? Would you dispose of me as easily?" Roger pointed to the body.

"No!" Anita collapsed on the floor in front of him. Her voice was small and smooth. "No, Roger. I will never get rid of you. You are my brother. The only one who has ever known the true me. I would die if I ever lost you."

Roger squatted next to her and patted her back. He knew he had to give in to Anita and hated it. The only way out of her grasp was after she died or a cure. It didn't matter to him which one. He wanted this nightmare to be over.

He asked Anita, "Do you have a plan?"

Anita turned and gave him a wide smile. "As a matter of fact, I do."

24 - Bailey

October 14, 2017

Mid-October gave little relief from the heat of summer. The days were slightly cooler, but the humidity stayed trapped in the ground. Bailey still found yard work unbearable. Of course, it didn't help to consider the neighbors would freak out once they saw the hedge pulled out.

The tree was gone but had done irreversible damage to the hedge. The Major and his wife had already commented on its shabby state and implied it must be "dealt with." Which Jordan and Bailey intended to do. But the heat...and the neighbors.

They ate breakfast together in mutual silence. Jordan was the first to speak as he broke apart his doughnut. "I'm kind of nervous going out there, but I can't stand to look at the mangled hedge."

"I know. Let's start after breakfast, work quickly, and then take the rest of the day off. It won't take long if we both work at it," Bailey said. She tried to make light of the situation, but it wasn't easy. She dreaded their exposure to Anita and Roger in the front yard while they tore the hedge out.

Bailey added, "We will tie up Alex in the front, under the tree. Maybe that will be enough of a menace to leave us alone." *But it wasn't Alex they needed to worry about.*

As if Jordan could read her mind, he said, "I don't want any trouble. I want to deal with the hedge and not be harassed. Are you sure the hedge is ours?"

"Jordan, you saw the survey. You measured it out. Yes, the hedge is ours," Bailey said a little too hastily. "Fuck the neighbors. If they were so worried, they would have done something about it already." Bailey was tired of the subject. She was tired of the neighbors.

Jordan squirmed a little in his chair. "The thought of peeling my wife off one of the neighbors makes me anxious. And your sharp tongue and snarky comments aren't always the best response. So, let's get this over."

Bailey knew she had poked the bear just a little too much. She redirected the conversation. "Do you want me to move the truck so we can load right into the bed?" she offered. "It might make things quicker. It isn't like we have a gorgeous lawn."

He smiled and popped a piece of doughnut in his mouth. "No, I think we'll be just fine. I'll cut down most of it with the brush hog attachment on the weed trimmer and maybe the chainsaw for the weed tree. You are sure it is a weed tree?"

"Yes, it is a weed tree. Until a couple of years ago, I treated it like one of the bushes. It wasn't one of the things planted there. I am sure of that."

"I'll measure the property line one more time, especially at the tree. I want to make sure the tree belongs to us."

Bailey bowed her head. "Okay. Let's get this over with."

#

They finished breakfast and headed outside to start their clearing project. Bailey tied Alex to the maple tree while Jordan went to the shed to gather the tools. She looked beyond the hedge and noted neither Roger's nor Anita's vehicles out front. She smiled and let out a sigh of relief.

She shifted her gaze to the carnage the massive pecan had created as it had fallen. But the hedge had always been overgrown. The previous owners of her house hadn't tended to the hedge at all. Now Bailey, in vain, had tried to control it. Either way, it was still a point of contention.

The barrier was a trimmed mixture of unhealthy privet, Virginia ivy, poison ivy, and a couple of weed trees that ran along the property line from the curb to the now four-foot diameter stump. The pecan tree and the hedge shielded her view into the neighbor's side windows and vice versa. As much as she was glad to see the hedge go, it meant she had to see Anita and Roger more. They would replant something when they had the money. So, she had instructed the crew to let the trunk fall on the hedge if it made it easier for them. And they took full advantage and left a pile of mangled mess.

Jordan came around the front of the house. Bailey turned and said, "We are in luck. It doesn't look like either of them is at home. So, let's do this thing." She clapped her hands, and they attacked the twenty-five feet of the mangled hedge.

Jordan and Bailey worked diligently to cut and strip away the first half of the hedge that drooped over their side yard. Jordan cut, and Bailey grabbed and hauled the debris away from the work area. Bailey ruminated while she worked. They had enjoyed these weekend yard improvement projects in the past, but today, she felt a different vibe. Today, it wasn't fun. Bailey wasn't sure it would ever be fun again. It made her sad and angry at the same time. The neighbors took that away from her.

A black BMW pulled up in front of the house next door. Jordan and Bailey held their breath. It was Roger's car. They continued to work as if no one was watching them.

25: Roger

October 14, 2017

Roger cut the engine as he sat and stared out the windshield. *What the fuck are they doing?* He sat and waited for a sign of what to do, but inspiration didn't come. Today, he needed to get rid of the two bodies he had stored in the garage. He didn't have time to deal with the neighbors. His stomach tightened, and he could feel the bile creep up his throat. Now, the panic had turned into rage. They cut down the whole hedge!

He yelled out, "Stop doing that! You don't know what the fuck you are doing! You are destroying everything!" *What would he do without the alder? How could he make the tonic? What about their privacy?*

"What the fuck are you doing?" Roger balled his fists and banged on the dashboard. "I have to call Anita. She'll know what to do." He gathered his paperwork from the front seat and opened the door. He hurried to the front door and never took his eyes off the neighbors. They never acknowledged him, which made his blood boil even more. He unlocked the front door, slammed it behind him, and ran for the phone. He dialed Anita's direct line at the university, and she picked up on the second ring.

"Anita Belo, how may I help you?"

"They are cutting the fucking bushes down!" Roger screamed into the phone.

"Do nothing. Don't say a thing. I will be home in a couple of minutes."

Roger hung up and went into the kitchen. He grabbed a martini glass and poured himself a stiff one. The top-shelf vodka smoothed the back of his throat perfectly. It was what he needed to calm his nerves. His mood changed, and the panic faded away, snuffed out by the vodka. He relished the scene that would play out in a couple of minutes. He knew it would be a scene because Anita was losing her mind. She wouldn't be able to control herself. She would make them stop.

Roger stepped back outside onto the front porch. He stood there with his arms crossed and stared at the neighbors. He talked to himself under his breath. "Idiots! You look stupid. Both of you are in the scorching sun, dirty, and doing manual labor. It must suck not making enough money to pay for some poor slob to do your dirty work." He straightened his collar and tie and continued smugly. "Just keep doing what you're doing. Anita is on her way."

Moments later, Anita pulled haphazardly into the driveway and jumped out. She didn't acknowledge Roger as she stomped over to the hedge. Roger jogged off the steps and joined her at the edge of their property. Jordan and Bailey continued to work.

"What are you doing?" Anita screamed. Jordan and Bailey didn't answer.

Anita continued to question. "What happened to the hedge? Why does it look like this? Are they going to come back and fix this?" Anita's arms flailed and sweat flew from her red face.

Roger stood behind her, out of the contact zone. He had seen his sister mad before and always ensured he stayed out of her path. He was glad her wrath wasn't towards him.

Jordan was the first to respond as he continued his task. "We are taking the bushes down because they are damaged. The tree people are not coming back." Bailey stopped her work and stood beside Jordan while Alex barked in the background.

"You mean they won't take care of the stump and fix the bushes?" Anita poked her finger at Jordan.

Jordan shot back. "No. Grinding the stump was extra. I didn't have extra because you went back on your word and didn't want to contribute to the cost of taking the tree down. The stump is staying. And as far as the bushes are concerned, they are out-of-control weeds. And they are damaged beyond repair. So, I am taking them down."

Anita's response was high-pitched, and she clipped each word. "Half are on our property. You can't take them down!"

Jordan took a deep breath. "No. I have shown you the survey. Hell, I gave you a copy of the survey!" He paused for another deep breath. "The hedges are on our property. If we want to take them down, we will."

Roger noticed Bailey had backed away. She grabbed the dog and leashed him. Roger's back stiffened. *Was she going to come over here?* While Anita continued to argue with Jordan, Roger watched Bailey go down the steps and down the street. Once she was out of sight, he let out his breath. *God, he hated dogs!*

Now that Bailey and the dog were gone, Roger only had to worry about Jordan. He hoped Anita wouldn't make it physical because he couldn't hold her back. Roger watched Jordan try to continue his work, but Anita kept up with her questions as Jordan worked. *Jordan was always more diplomatic than Bailey. Maybe they could talk Jordan into an agreement.*

Jordan stopped and leaned on his shovel. "Anita, I have gone over this several times, and you standing there yelling at me isn't going to change my decision."

"This is harassment! I am going to call the cops!" Anita huffed and puffed.

"Fine, call the cops. You are yelling at me about my work on my property. I'm sure Helen and Bella will be witnesses to that fact." Jordan pointed over his shoulder at the two women across the street. "Let the cops decide who is harassing whom!"

Roger stepped away in anticipation of going and calling the cops but stopped when he saw Anita pause. Had she remembered the bodies in the garage that he hadn't buried yet? The last thing they needed was cops coming to their house.

In silence, Roger and Anita glared at Jordan as he continued to dig. Roger shifted around, unable to stand still. The tension was thick, and everything seemed to move in slow motion. He watched Anita as she paced back and forth along the property line. She mumbled to herself, but Roger couldn't hear what she said.

This stalemate lasted ten minutes until Bailey and the dog showed up. Their appearance seemed to activate Anita's rage again. She yelled, "This has been very stressful on us. Do you know how much sleep I've lost over this tree thing?" She waved her hand toward the stump.

Bailey rushed to the part of the hedge that remained. Her face now was beet red, too. "Stressful for you? Are you fucking kidding me? You two are making it unbearable to even walk out of our house! We tried to do the right thing. But that wasn't good enough!"

"The light shines into my window, and the sound of the traffic is dreadful!" Anita said. She sounded like a little child.

Roger wasn't sure if Anita would charge like a bull or melt like an ice cube. He had to do something before she did. "We will get a fence built!" he exclaimed. "Can't you at least leave some hedges until that is done?" Roger looked at Anita. The idea of a fence seemed to surprise her but calmed her.

Jordan's voice was again smooth. "A fence? We can't afford to put up a fence."

Roger rushed to explain. "No, we will pay for it."

Everyone was silent. Roger took a deep breath. Was this the answer that would make them happy? He kicked himself for not thinking of it beforehand.

Jordan said, "Fine. If you want me to leave that half of the bushes, I will." He pointed to the half of the hedge that hung over their yard.

Roger rushed to the stump of the freshly cut alder and said, "And nothing past this point." He motioned to the far side of the alder and the hedge untouched by the pecan.

Jordan said, "Fine, nothing past that point, and as far as those bushes are concerned, I will leave them until you get your fence built. Then we will take them down because they're ours."

26: Roger

October 14, 2017

Satisfied with the ceasefire, Anita and Roger retreated into their cool, dark living room. He made her tea and sent her off to bed for a nap. Meanwhile, he gathered his nerves to go out and bury the two bodies stored in the garage. As much as he wanted to drink himself into the bottom of a vodka bottle, he needed his wits to finish the dirty task.

Roger opened the back door and stepped out onto the patio. With a deep breath, he searched for any scent of decay. He ensured there was no odor and surveyed the backyard for the best cover from prying eyes. Close to the back fence provided the best cover. Though the neighbors took the front hedge down, there was still plenty of overgrowth in the backyard. *God, he hated yard work.*

He hesitated at the garage door. There, he could smell the rotten flesh. His stomach turned, and bile filled his mouth. *Shit!* Roger spat it out, took a deep breath, and opened the door. He quickly found the shovel and exited the garage before he exhaled. Outside the garage, he bent over and panted, his face wet with sweat.

Roger gave up the fight for clean clothes, and it didn't take long before his tracksuit was covered with dirt and sweat. He cursed the current situation and the fact that he was knee-deep in soil. *This wasn't a task for a civilized man.*

After Anita died, he would throw away his work clothes and put this all behind him. Everything hinged on Anita. It always had. And Roger did what he was told. He always did. It depressed him. He had a career and an image of the man he wanted to be, but he still relied on Anita for emotional support, even after all these years. She was still his lifeline, and he hated that fact. He yearned to detach himself from her and be out on his own. He knew the life he had known would die if Anita were gone.

Anita was his big sister, and he owed his life to her. She had saved him from their mother and the virus, but…

If he left, Anita would view it as an act of treason. As the disease set in, he feared she would become crazy enough to hunt him down and kill him too. Like a scorned lover, if she couldn't have him, no one would.

The thought made Roger shudder. "When are you going to die?" he whispered.

Those uttered words made his heart sink. It wasn't the first time he had said those words. He had whispered those exact words all the nights that led to his mother's death. So many nights, he and Anita hid in the closet and watched their mother slowly go insane. And finally, she was gunned down in her own bedroom.

Roger's eyes welled up with tears. "I'm hiding in the closet again," he said.

In the garage, he wrestled with the two bodies. His mind raced, and his emotions swung wildly. As he wrapped the bodies in plastic, his grief turned to anger. He kicked "the experiment" in the stomach and felt his foot sink deep into the flesh. He growled and kicked it again because it felt good. Then he dropped to his knees.

"No, no, no…." Roger shook his head in regret. Apathy and emptiness festered in him like the disease killing his sister. The only emotion he could express was anger. He was mad at the world and the people who had betrayed him. And himself. Yet, he knew that he could leave his sister if he had a set of balls.

He stroked the top of the plastic-wrapped body. "How lucky you are to be released from this world."

How much longer could he do this?

Alex, the scrappy terrier next door, interrupted Roger's internal rant. The dog stood silently at the edge of the backyard hedge and watched Roger through a small bare spot in the bushes. And he would growl, bark, and wag his tail every so often. Roger remained still and hoped the owners would call off the mangy mutt. Today, that damn dog was insistent. *Please don't come over here.*

Roger hated dogs, and in turn, the dogs knew it. Each time a dog was close, the beast would bark, growl, and try to lunge at Roger. It reminded him of the war-torn Angola of his childhood. *Dogs were the devil on earth.*

Damn it. Roger mumbled, "Not today. I need to get the bodies in the ground before they start to melt."

Alex continued to bark. Roger could hear the neighbors as they called to the dog, but the dog refused to give up. He rustled the leaves at his feet, hoping the neighbors would see him and go back inside. The scene from that morning flashed in his head.

"The alder. Why did you have to cut down the alder? Why not wait just a little longer?"

He looked down at the two bodies and kicked them into the shallow graves.

27: Roger

October 15, 2017

While Roger dug in the dirt and got rid of the two bodies, Anita decided her experiment with the study group had failed. She then declared she needed a different type of person to experiment with, someone they could keep at the house so she could focus on their progress.

Roger was appalled by the lengths Anita would go to in her quest. Moreover, he was amazed at how easily he gave up and gave in to her ideas. Two people were dead, and Anita's new plans still seemed like business as usual. They spent much of Saturday evening at the kitchen table, focused on a strategy that suited Anita's needs and didn't freak Roger out completely.

Almost two weeks after Anita frantically stormed through the university quad, she was back with Roger to hunt for new guinea pigs. They found a bench that gave them a full view of the courtyard. She acted giddy, and this made Roger nervous. He distracted himself away from Anita's mood and replayed yesterday's conversation in his head.

"What about the six remaining students you gave candy to?" he asked.

"They will have to fend for themselves."

"What the hell, Anita! They are human beings."

"Roger. Six people getting sick with an undetermined disease in a cesspool called college life isn't that unusual." She'd waved her hand at an invisible fly. "Hell, most officials will be happy it is only six and not a full-blown outbreak!"

"But…"

"Enough about them, Roger. We need to decide who we want next."

Roger watched Anita's expression turn from an angry, mad scientist to a hopeful researcher. He bowed his head and took a deep breath. It will soon be over if you go along with her and her scheme.

"I think I want a male subject," she went on. "I've always wanted to boss around men. It is powerful to give them a taste of what they have done to women in the past."

Roger scuffed. Lord, help us all.

"Or… maybe we should look for a female. You know, something for you, my dear brother." She leaned over and squeezed his cheek.

Roger reared back. "I do just fine for myself."

"Sorry. It's just that you don't get out much. Especially in the last couple of weeks…." Anita stopped and let a small smile appear on her face. "Wait a second…you have someone! Why haven't you ever introduced us? You should bring her over." Anita's face lit up with excitement. She crossed her arms and nodded. "It all makes sense now. You disappear for hours and come back in a good mood…."

Roger felt the heat of embarrassment warm his cheeks. This is the reason! He screamed in his head. He took a deep breath to calm himself, straightened the cuffs of his shirt, and cleared his throat. "It is none of your business. Could we please remain on the topic?"

"Oh, we are, Roger. You're the topic now. I wasn't entirely sure if you even like girls. Wait! You're gay!" she said in excitement and clapped her hands together. "Well, that would explain a lot. All those secret errands you run off to."

Roger snapped back. "I'm not gay! And you know nothing about me or my life!"

Roger shook his head at the memory, which caused a wave of nausea. He leaned forward, rested his elbows on his knees, and cupped his forehead with his hands. *I regretted yesterday's booze fest and today's consequences.* Typically, he had a handle on the vodka, but the drama in the morning, the manual work in the afternoon, and the lack of water had created a perfect storm of a hangover.

They sat and watched the parade of students pass for an hour. They said nothing to each other. They only exchanged elbow nudges and headshakes at potential candidates. Anita looked fully engaged in the scene while Roger slipped into his recurring fantasy world, where he was a high roller at a blackjack table in Vegas. Today, the made-up life bored him. His cell buzzed and knocked him back into the present before he dug it out of his pocket and read the text message.

He shook his head. *Not now.*

Anita leaned over and tried to get a glimpse of the screen. "Anything wrong?"

He quickly replied, 'Not now.' Then, he deleted the text and turned the phone to airplane mode. *Bye-bye Vegas.* Now, he had two problems at hand. He looked and met Anita's eyes, but she had refocused away from his cell phone.

Anita wiggled on the bench. "Can't one loner come by so we can snatch him up?"

"Stop being impatient." He was impatient too, but he chose not to show it. "Maybe this isn't the best way," Roger said. "Maybe we should think about Plan B."

Anita didn't ask what Plan B was. Instead, she pouted. "Why can't anything be easy?"

He looked at her from the corner of his eye. He was unclear about what to make of the immature Anita. It was annoying. *Was this how it was to have children?* No wonder Father had always been pissed. Now Roger understood why he'd left for a year.

"I don't mean to be annoying," Anita said flatly.

Roger turned and looked at her. *Did she just read his mind?* "No, you are fine. But, if you want a more focused experiment, we should take a more proactive approach to the selection. Get them into a position where we can ask questions. Then weed out those that won't work."

"Have any ideas?" She didn't give Roger a chance to respond. Anita's eye was distracted by a young, thin boy with red hair and bright blue eyes. "Oh, what about him? He's cute just sitting there alone."

Roger turned to look at the young man, and Anita swatted him. "Don't look directly at him. We don't want to scare him!"

Roger chuckled. "He doesn't even see us. We're old, remember. It's like we are Scrooge in *A Christmas Carol*. We are invisible. Trust me, that kid doesn't even know we exist." He let that comment sink in before continuing. "Don't you think you should look for someone more like us? Or what you are, at least?"

Anita crossed her arms and swiveled towards Roger while her face changed from curious to defensive. "Interesting question. What would you have in mind? Someone old like me, female, Portuguese, or maybe you mean someone who is from Angola?"

"Well, I was thinking all of those things. If we want a cure for your illness, wouldn't it make sense to find a prototype that mimics you, the end user?" Roger wasn't sure how that was going to fly. He was quick to continue while she sat quietly. "If you dive deep and focus on saving one type of person, someone with our heritage, perhaps you could *then* adjust it and apply it to everyone else."

Roger had shown little interest in Anita's research before. He had let himself glaze over and mentally slip away when she talked. It only brought up painful memories of his childhood. But as he sat there, he thought the solution could kill two birds with one stone.

"Roger, you are full of ideas. This isn't a bad one, but where do we find a Portuguese woman in her 50s?" Anita asked.

"Now, there's my specialty. I know where lonely women hang out, looking for a way out of their life." Roger smiled. *Most of the women he had known.*

Anita looked at him inquisitively. "Do tell, brother. Do tell."

28: Roger

October 15, 2017 - Earl's Place, Charlotte, North Carolina

In certain circles of Charlotte, Roger was known as a big spender. But, of course, these circles were in places where owning your car and having a well-paying job elevated you to the high class. To him, though, the admiration sufficed. It didn't matter who gave it to him. He was better than they were, which was what mattered. So, he was on a side street that separated the nice part of town from the questionable side.

While Roger drove, he second-guessed the decision to invite his sister into his private world. He wasn't sure how she would take it, and he didn't want to listen to her snarky comments. He didn't have to justify his life. She did what she needed to get through the night. He did what he needed.

"Where are we going?" she asked.

"A place I know."

"Roger, I'm seeing another mysterious side to you," she said as she ran her hand along his arm.

He put his hand on her knee but pulled back quickly when he remembered it was his sister in the passenger's seat. He tried to cover up the awkward moment. "When we get inside, let me do the talking. They know me here. Okay, Anita?"

This morning, Roger suggested they wear their best go-to church clothes to make them feel they were on top of the world. And even though she was sick with an incurable disease, Anita looked lovely. It wouldn't take long before they picked what they wanted.

Roger turned into a dirt parking lot and parked on the side of a windowless cinderblock building labeled Earl's Place with sad neon signs announcing their beer selections. Roger rounded the car and opened the door for Anita. He felt like he was in his full-fledged James Bond mode and had to execute his role to the highest degree. He walked arm in arm with her across the gravel and opened the door.

Sunlight flooded the interior and cut through the dark, stale atmosphere like a knife. They stepped in and let the door close behind them, and the room went back into the dim light. Only the people in the bar looked in their direction. On one long wall, the bar took up two-thirds of the room. Video games lined the far wall, and small tables and cheap banquet chairs cluttered the rest of the space. A few tables had couples who sat close and whispered. Half the bar stools were full, but no one seemed to be together.

"Roger Moore, good to see you!" the bartender yelled.

Anita snickered under her breath. "Roger Moore? You have got to be kidding. Is that what you told them your name was? Do they not know who played James Bond?"

Another ping of regret coursed through Roger. This was the wrong part of town for Anita. "Shut up. And let me do the talking," he hissed under his breath, but he kept a smile plastered on his lips.

They moved deeper into the bar and chose two bar stools halfway down the row. Roger ordered for the both of them, and they waited patiently as the bartender started to shoot the shit.

"Roger. It's been a while. And now you show up with such a pretty lady." The bartender let the sentence drift off as he winked at Anita.

Roger winced at the gesture because he knew Anita hated people who winked. They reminded her of used car salesmen or, worse yet, their father. Anita wiggled on her stool, and Roger clamped a hand on her knee to force her to settle down. She stopped her bottom adjustment and let her eyes roam the room.

Roger watched Anita for her telltale micro-expressions of disapproval. She leaned forward and whispered, "What a horrible place."

Roger swiveled to take in the full grandeur of the dive bar. The walls were decorated with old posters of sports heroes and movie stars, but none appeared to be from this decade. The bar's favorite famous figures were John Wayne, Robert Redford, John McEnroe, and Joe Montana. *Horrible indeed. It was a sad place but a great place to catch a sucker.*

The bartender appeared with her white wine and another wink. Roger noticed her upper lip twitch. He chuckled to himself; *Anita hated people who winked.* He watched Anita take a long draw off her wine and followed her gaze to a woman at the far end of the bar. As soon as Roger made eye contact, the woman approached.

"Roger, baby, you never come around here anymore." The tanned woman leaned against the bar and tried to act casual but just looked drunk. Then, finally, she said, "Baby. I've been looking for you."

Hopefully, she isn't as drunk as she looks. Roger held out his arm, and the woman curled into it. Roger saw Anita draw her Christian Louboutin shoes away from the lady.

"Baby, aren't you going to introduce me?" Her expression changed from cloudy to focused as she looked at Anita. "Hey, you look like me," she said as she pointed to Anita and then to herself.

She stood beside Roger with her left arm wrapped around his neck. She stared at Anita and then reached out to touch her. Anita recoiled. "Hey, I'm not going to hurt you," the woman slurred.

Anita asked, "Roger, aren't you going to introduce us?" she asked in a proper tone.

"Cherry, this is my sister, Ann," Roger said. He noted the disgust on Anita's face because he knew she hated the nickname Ann. He took a big gulp of his beer.

Anita reached out to shake her hand, "It is nice to meet you, Cherry."

Cherry recoiled, then laughed. "Oh, I'm just kidding you. It is very nice to meet you, too." And she ended with a bit of a wobbly curtsy.

"So, Cherry, have you known Roger long?" Anita asked with just a little venom.

Cherry ruffled the top of Roger's head. "I've known this guy for a couple of years now. He's my John McEnroe." She put her nose close to his ear and purred.

Anita pulled the rest of the wine out of the glass with one swig. The bartender was quick to offer her another wine. "No. I will have a vodka on the rocks." She swiveled back to Cherry. "Your John McEnroe?" Anita asked.

"Yeah, he looks like the tennis player. And I just love it when he wears those tight little white shorts." Cherry was trying to pinch his butt but couldn't catch hold.

Anita nearly spat out her newly delivered drink. But, instead, she smiled at Roger. Anita looked like she was enjoying herself, whereas Roger felt increasingly uncomfortable. Finally, Anita's eyes refocused, and Roger knew that meant she was bored. *Time is a-wasting.*

"Sherry," Anita started.

"Cherry, like the fruit," the drunk woman said.

"What?"

"My name. I like to pronounce it like the fruit. Roger says I should elevate my status and life station by spelling it Cherrie, with an I-E, not Cherry, but I like the fruit name."

Wow, that didn't make any sense.

Anita cracked her neck to release the pressure. "Cherry. Would you like to get out of here and maybe have some home cooking?"

Roger shot Anita a look. *Way not to be subtle.*

"Oh my god, are you talking like fried chicken and biscuits? I love biscuits!" She released her grip on Roger and hugged Anita. As she continued the embrace, Cherry's lower body danced in place. "Ann, you are like my new best BFF." Cherry grabbed Anita's arm and pulled her off the stool. "Come on. Let's get out of here and get some food."

Roger drained the beer and placed the money needed to cover the bill on the bar. He looked at the bartender, and he winked. The bartender chuckled and smiled like he knew what would happen tonight.

Roger shook his head. *If only you knew.*

29: Roger

October 15, 2017 - Leroy's Chicken Shack, Charlotte, North Carolina

The dinner debate continued as they settled into the car. Roger noted Cherry liked the idea of home cooking but was just as happy with Leroy's Chicken Shack. He didn't want to cook, so he headed to Leroy's for greasy fried chicken and added a stop at the liquor store. Unfortunately, Anita's plan wouldn't work unless Roger had a lot of alcohol.

Roger wondered if he had played his hand a little too hard. He wanted to get rid of Cherry and end the relationship. She had become too clingy and full of questions. She wanted to learn about the true Roger Moore; it was the last thing he wanted. When Roger needed a peaceful place to land, Cherry fit that need. But now, he wanted something newer. He had to shake loose of Cherry first.

Roger had already picked out his new lover, another lady from the bar, and he was relieved to see she wasn't at Earl's tonight. The drama of three women at once frightened him. A train wreck of a situation Roger was not prepared to tackle. It would have been a disaster, which would have fucked up the future. Instead, Roger's mind jumped to the big question.

What was the future for him? How much longer did Anita indeed have?

Anita showed signs of the last stage of the disease already.

From here, it would be a quick downhill trajectory. In less than a month, he might not be in Charlotte. After Anita died, he could go anywhere and be with anyone. He was happy to be closing this chapter of his life tonight. *Goodbye to Earl's, goodbye to Cherry.*

"Don't do the drive thru. There are three cars in line." Cherry leaned forward between the front seats of Roger's BMW and pointed to the queue. "It's quicker to go in." She hiccupped at the end of the statement, and a waft of stale beer blew by his ear.

"Roger, Cherry seems to know what she is talking about. Look, there is a space right there," she said. Anita smiled over her shoulder at Cherry.

He sighed as he pulled in and parked the car. The door flew open and banged the car in the next space. "Shit!" Roger expected a comment from Anita but got no response. With a slam of the door, he hurried across the parking lot. The two of them in the car alone made him nervous.

#

Anita watched him disappear into the restaurant before she turned to face Cherry in the back seat. "I never knew that about the drive-thru line." Anita regulated her voice, so she didn't sound condescending.

"Yeah. I worked at Burger King. It's one of those things they tell you," Cherry announced.

"They, meaning who?" Anita didn't care. She just wanted to keep Cherry engaged so she could study the behavior of her newest lab rat.

"Who?"

"You said 'they.' Who are they?" Anita saw the blank look on Cherry's face and sighed. "Who told you this fascinating bit of information about the drive-thru?" Anita narrowed her eyes and willed Cherry to form a coherent thought. *I don't have time for this.*

"You know, I'm not sure. I just always knew it. Maybe I made it up." Cherry laughed at her own joke. "I guess that would make me 'those' people." Cherry frowned and fidgeted with the safety belt.

Anita stared at Cherry and saw a drunk, skanky version of herself. The resemblance was creepy. At that moment, Anita realized she knew little about Roger's private life. She wasn't sure if she felt flattered or appalled by her brother's choice of lovers.

"Cherry, tell me a little about yourself."

"Oh, isn't much to tell. What would you like to know?" Cherry asked as she stared out the window. Anita thought she looked like a puppy waiting for its owner to return.

"Let's start with something simple, like how did you meet Roger?" Anita looked towards the restaurant to see if Roger was in sight. She needed more time to get details.

"Oh, we met at the bar—Earl's. My jerk boyfriend at the time was roughing me up. Roger got up, grabbed his tennis racket, and backhanded the asshole across the room. It's funny thinking about it." Cherry smiled at the memory.

"He had a tennis racket with him?" Anita pressed. Roger didn't play tennis.

"Yes, and he looked so cute in his white tennis shorts." Cherry's smile grew even bigger.

Anita smiled, but for a different reason. *Cherry, you're an idiot. Roger in white tennis shorts.* She had never seen him in shorts at all. *It must have been for the look.* Cherry gave no more details, but Anita imagined the scene. What a scene it must have been. She was proud at the thought that Roger showed a backbone. *You go, Roger. Be the king of your jungle.*

Anita hurried the conversation forward. "You said backhand. Are you a tennis player too?"

"I used to be. I played in high school. I made it to the state championships my junior year."

Wow! The first complete and coherent sentence.

Cherry continued. "It was a long time ago." And the haziness was back. Finally, Cherry stopped talking and stared out the window.

30: Roger

October 15, 2017

They sat around the dining table, ate fried chicken and mashed potatoes, and drank vodka. Cherry talked a lot, as she always did while she was drunk. But, as usual, Roger didn't listen. He never did. He watched Anita stalk her prey. She was in her element right now. *But did she channel the brilliant researcher Roger knew she was, or had she become a complete savage?*

"Roger, can I see you in the kitchen?" Anita excused herself, and Roger followed. As soon as they turned the corner, she grabbed him. "How much longer before Cherry passes out?"

Damn, for a sick person, she's got a good grip. He pulled her fingers away to release her clasp. "I don't know."

"You don't know? I thought you were lovers. Cherry made it sound like you have been together for a while. You can't tell me you had sex with her when she wasn't drunk." Anita's whisper became louder.

Roger snapped back. "What the hell does that mean? You're implying I'm not good enough to take someone to bed without alcohol?" He tried to push beyond Anita, but she blocked his move and grabbed him again.

"No. That's not what I meant at all."

She tried to stroke his cheek, but he grabbed her wrist. He had had enough of the charade. "Get to the point, Anita." His voice was cold and sharp.

"Ow! Let go, Roger. You're hurting me." It was now her turn to dig out of his grasp.

"Now, Anita!" he said through clenched teeth.

Her voice turned into a high-pitched whine. "When I woke up this morning…" Anita cleared her throat. Her voice was normal and concise. "When I woke up this morning, I wanted to make damn sure it would be a great day. And now I'm in my dining room with my beloved brother and this wonderful new person. It's been a great day, but now it's time to work."

Roger gave up trying to be quiet. "Focus, Anita! What do you want me to do?"

"I need you to have sex with her. And keep her in bed, preferably passed out."

Roger's shoulders slumped, and he turned back into the dining room. *Sex with Cherry while Anita lurked…It would be the worst lay he would ever have.*

#

Lucky for Roger, as soon as Cherry settled in his bed, she passed out. But he didn't let Anita know. Instead, Roger took the time to regroup and contemplate his next move. Could he let Anita harm Cherry? *Anita wasn't going to hurt Cherry. Right?*

He lay down beside Cherry and stroked her cheek. *You can call the whole thing off,* his heart screamed, but his head told him it needed to be done for the greater good. So he leaned over, kissed her lips lightly, and then got off the bed.

Even in the dark, the room glowed from the lights on the street. Roger undressed and draped his clothes over the side chair in the corner. Then, with a deep sigh, he opened the door to the hallway. Anita waited in a chair outside the door. She wiggled with excitement.

"Well, that was quick," she smirked as she blew by him into the bedroom.

Roger followed her back into the room but stopped at the doorway. "I'll get the bed ready in the laundry room."

"No. I want you here with me."

"Why?" He was exhausted, and he could hear it in his question. *Did Anita notice? Did he care if she did?*

"I need an assistant," she said in a whisper.

"Anita." *Why must I be a part of this?*

"I know you don't want to help. But the least you can do is stay close just in case…."

"Just in case, what?" He was tired, drunk, and a little nauseous. He slid along the wall and stood in the corner, cloaked by a heavy shadow. Anita pulled a vial and a syringe from her pocket, and Roger felt a panic rush up his spine. *God, did she have it in her pocket the whole time? He could have been stabbed!*

Roger's heartbeat thumped in his ears like a giant clock ticking off the seconds. He watched, frozen, as Anita knelt on the bed and glided the needle into Cherry's arm. Her reaction was immediate and violent. A field of small red bumps flowered around the injection point, and Cherry sat straight up in bed. Her eyes were wide but not focused. When she opened her mouth to speak, what spewed out was vomit.

Anita bounced back and screamed. "Roger! Come help me!"

Roger rushed to the bed and grabbed Cherry by the shoulders. Her back was rigid, and it took all his strength to force her back onto the pillows. She stared up at Roger as she grasped her throat with one hand and his arm with her other.

"Jesus, Anita, she can't breathe! How much did you give her?"

He climbed on the bed and straddled Cherry. "What are you doing, just standing there? Help her!"

Cherry convulsed under his hold. Blood oozed out of her nose and mouth. She took one gasp of air before she went limp. Anita turned on the bedside light and shuffled off the bed. She stood, frozen, with the needle in her hands. Roger felt for a pulse, then jumped off the bed and lunged at Anita. He caught her by the throat and pushed his sister up against the wall.

"What the fuck did you do? She's dead!"

Anita opened her mouth, but nothing came out. Her eyes were wide with shock. Roger stared at her. "This changes everything," he said with a hiss. He released his hold on his sister and stormed out of the room.

#

Sleep for Roger was restless, at best. He was utterly exhausted after he put Cherry's body in the garage and cleaned his room of the smell of vomit and death. But despite the drama the night before, he woke up as usual before daybreak.

A couple of days ago, he had had so many opportunities. Now, this morning, all those doors were closed. First, Cherry's death triggered empathy for her and the two before her. Then, sometime during the night, it dawned on him that he had killed them all.

How had this eluded him until now? What was he doing?

He thought about the assumptions people would make. From the outside, it looked like he was a monster, and Anita was his keeper. It was really the opposite, but it hadn't started that way. He and Anita had begun this journey with lots of love and dedication for each other. But Cherry changed all of that. He realized now that Anita was only in it for herself. Roger wasn't her brother anymore. To Anita, he was collateral damage. Was he not worthy of her love?

He frowned. Even if Cherry recovered, who's to say she wouldn't have gone to the police? The consequence never presented itself with the two previous experiments, now dead and buried in the backyard. *And what was the status of the other six?*

Roger pondered the consequences if they spoke up. He tapped down his fear by concluding that even if they went to the police, it wouldn't cause too much stink. Their delusional stories would be brushed off as a nasty by-product of some unknown virus. Anita had gone so far as to do things differently each time. If anyone paid attention, no two stories would be the same.

Alone in his crappy bed, in this crappy house, in this crappy city, he had nothing to show for his life. *Was that Anita's fault?* Going to Germany as children wasn't their decision, but as an adult, he didn't have to follow Anita in her lifelong quest to cure Bat Crap Fever. He didn't have to be so needy for her love and approval. And he certainly hadn't had to introduce Cherry to his sister or let her use her as a lab rat. *Cherry's death is all on you, Roger.* He rolled over, punched the pillows, and thought of Anita. He wanted to hurt her physically, like she had hurt him emotionally. But it still wasn't the right time.

Roger got up, did a quick workout, showered, dressed in his best suit, and left before Anita woke. He needed to get out of the house. He needed to think away from all this madness. In his BMW, Roger sat, hands on the wheel, his head back. He wanted to get away, far away. But he sat there and stared at the house.

Was it finally time to leave her? Could he break free from her neediness?

He smiled at the thought. He didn't care anymore; mentally, he was already gone. Anita was on her own. He only needed to point the car at the sunset and never look back.

31: Kurt

October 17, 2017

It was 12:35 p.m. on a crisp October afternoon, but Kurt wasn't in the mood to enjoy it. He felt edgy and sick. *Great, not even a month into fall, and I caught a cold.* Other students in the study group had been ill. *Had he caught what they had?*

He was interrupted by a voice from the front of the lecture hall, "Mr. Holloway, what is the common term used to describe a …?" The instructor's voice faded as Kurt's attention returned to how sick he felt. Professor Anita Belo stood at the front of the room with her hands on her hips as she waited for an answer.

"Bat Crap Crazy," he mumbled. *The only thing between me and my degree is this nut job.*

She interrupted again. "Mr. Holloway, I am waiting." Her voice was dry as chalk dust.

His stomach turned, and beads of sweat rolled down the back of his neck. *I'm going to throw up.*

"I'm not feeling so hot," Kurt chirped as he hastily packed up and stood. Dizziness blossomed in his head as he headed for the door.

"Email me later for the assignment," Anita said after him as he stumbled out of the classroom.

#

Kurt woke up face down on the cold bathroom floor in his apartment. He tried to recall he'd gotten home, but his memory was blank. He rolled over and stared at the ceiling, and an image of Anita's sick face appeared.

"Why the hell was she smiling?" he said out loud.

He shook his head to clear out the image, which only produced a wave of nausea. Once it passed, he crawled into a standing position and turned the water on to brush his teeth. The water flow put him in a trance, and he sang along with the water, "Oh, I love the rainy nights, love the rainy nights…." Kurt stopped singing.

I shouldn't know that John Davidson sang that song on his variety show.

Kurt's phone vibrated, dinged, and knocked him back to the present. He read the text, "Call me now at 704-555-2378. A. Belo."

I don't think so. Crazy bitch.

Kurt turned off the water. He went back and flopped on the bed. The golden light of late afternoon streamed through his window. *What time was it anyway?* He looked down at the home screen. 4:45 p.m. He took one more glance at the text. *Homework and study groups would have to wait.*

Kurt tossed and turned for a good half hour with no sound sleep. He was exhausted and wired. He dripped with sweat, but he froze to the bone. His stomach was calm now, but he shuddered at how vile he had felt earlier. He feared the feeling would be back as soon as he moved. So, he didn't.

If you call Belo now, you can get the homework. Remember, only two months before graduation.

Kurt moaned at the thought but knew he had to call. He sat up, searched for his phone, and found it beside him. It lit up with a starry background and displayed 5:30 p.m. as the current time. He hit redial and waited.

"This is Professor Belo," Anita answered on the second ring.

"Professor Belo, this is Kurt Holloway from your …"

Anita cut him off, "Yes, yes, I know who you are. I have been waiting for your call." She continued, "Sorry about being abrupt. I am just concerned because you left the lecture so suddenly."

"Well…" Kurt paused. *Was this such a good idea?* "I wasn't feeling good. And…I was pretty sure no one wanted to witness what happened next…. So anyway, I just called to find out the homework for the next class."

"Do you want to meet? I have some handouts to give you."

"Um, could you just email them to me?"

"I could do that, but I should review them with you. You know, if you have questions." Her tone changed when she continued, "Kurt, do you have anyone to look after you at home? Could I swing by and bring you some soup? You should keep your intake of fluids up so you don't get dehydrated."

Why did Belo sound motherly?

"Kurt, are you still there?" she questioned.

"Yeah, I'm still here. Not sure I'm up for visitors. Plus, I wouldn't want to get you sick." *Nice. Always make it about her.*

"Listen, I understand. I appreciate you worrying about me. Why don't I come over? Drop the soup and the papers off at your door and leave? We can go over them tomorrow with a call."

"Um, I guess that would be alright. And thank you." *I have nothing in the house to eat, anyway.* He gave her his address and hung up. Kurt knew it was a bad decision, but he was hungry, tired, and didn't want to argue with her.

32: Anita

October 17, 2017 - Kurt's Apartment, Charlotte, North Carolina

Half an hour later, Anita and Roger arrived at Kurt's apartment building. Roger parked the BMW station wagon in front of a set of basic structures. They reminded Anita of the style of 1970s military barracks, solid but with no decorative details.

"I hope he lives on the first floor," Anita said.

"What?"

Anita shifted in the passenger's seat and looked at Roger. "I hope he lives on the first floor, or it's going to be more difficult to get the body out."

"Hmm."

Anita was annoyed that Roger wasn't more engaged. She continued to talk despite it. "So, the game plan is to convince him to let me in and ensure he eats the soup. As soon as the drugs take effect, I will call you to help me bring him out."

She looked out over the courtyard. She didn't like the situation. Her upper lip twitched with nervousness. There were too many windows and too many opportunities for people to see their strange activity. She hadn't planned the kidnapping very well. There wasn't any time. Anita feared the virus put Kurt on an accelerated path to death. She needed that data before he died.

Roger picked up the vibe. He reached out and put his hand on her shoulder. "If you have a problem, knock him out. Then we'll carry him out under the ruse of helping him to the hospital."

She turned back and smiled. "You always have the best ideas. Thank you for being so supportive. Kurt is going to be the one. I can feel it. He's going to be the last one."

Roger smiled back. "Seeing you in such a light mood is good. I hope he is the last one. Now, go get him." He fist-bumped her arm like a football coach.

She took a deep breath, sighed, and opened the door. Anita took the papers and the soup and headed to the door. Inside the vestibule, she was relieved to see Kurt's unit was on the first floor before her. She knocked and waited.

Anita became dizzy and leaned against the door frame as blood rushed through her body, from head to toe. *Was Kurt feeling the same way?* The thought sparked panic. She banged on the door again.

I have to get into the apartment.

"Kurt? Are you in there? Are you okay?" She held her ear close to the door and willed him to answer. "Kurt?" she called again.

"Yeah, I am okay. Just leave the stuff, and I'll get it." His voice was weak and right at the door. This perked up Anita a little. All she needed was a couple of inches, and she could find the strength to overtake him.

"You don't sound well. Let me come in."

"Um, I don't want to give you whatever I have, whatever it is."

Anita heard a thump. "Kurt? Are you okay? You really sound weak. I am right here. I can get you to the hospital if you need it." *You are being too helpful.* Anita checked the doorknob as she calmed her breathing down. *You're so close.*

"My head… Maybe I do need to go to the hospital.… But don't think it's tainted meat." Kurt's voice trailed off.

Anita was almost too giddy. She waited and calculated where Kurt was in the symptom timeline. With the presence of confusion and delusion, he was already in the second stage of the disease.

Kurt continued, but his voice was fainter. "I think the others died…I don't want to die."

"Let me help you."

She turned the handle and opened the door when she heard the lock release. She saw the young man curled up in the fetal position on the floor.

"Do you live alone?" Anita asked. She took in the room.

Kurt grunted. "Yeah."

She smiled. It was going to be more straightforward than she had hoped. "Oh, you look awful. Let me feel your head." She put the papers and soup down and reached for his forehead, but he shied away.

Anita pursed her lips in frustration and tried to reach for him again. *So close. Don't put up a fight now.* "Come on, let me feel your head." She touched his forehead. He was burning up. D*id she feed him too much of the virus, like with Cherry? Or had the virus mutated again?*

He had sped up symptoms she couldn't explain. She needed to get him back to the house for a thorough examination. A wave of nausea overcame her, and she leaned back to steady herself in the door frame.

Kurt said, "Do I look that bad?"

Your eyes are watery and red. Your skin is milky white and plastic-looking—the second stage.

She regained her composure. "No, I am just surprised by how warm you are. I'm going to take you to the hospital." She stood and added before he could protest, "And I will not take no for an answer." She stepped over him, turned her back, and dialed Roger's cell.

"Roger, I need your help. Kurt is very sick, and we must get him to the hospital." She hung up and marveled at the situation. For a single male who lived alone, it might take weeks for anyone to realize he was gone. And then, Anita turned back to Kurt. "Roger is my husband. He's out in the car and will help me help you." At the door, she watched Roger trot up the sidewalk to the front door and into the building.

Anita stood in the doorway, hands on her hips. They didn't greet each other. Instead, he handed her a pair of gloves and a white cloth. She put on gloves, wiped down everything she had touched, and shoved the papers into the bag with the soup.

Kurt lay still on the floor with his eyes closed. Roger got behind him and propped him up into a sitting position. Roger grunted, and Anita said, "Kurt, you must help us a little. You can't be dead yet."

A slip of the tongue.

But Kurt didn't seem to notice. He had passed out. Roger looked at her with disapproving eyes. "I need your help, Anita. I can't do this alone," Roger whined.

She huffed, "Fine!" Then, she stuffed the white cloth into her coat pocket and grabbed Kurt's left arm. "Ready? On three. One, two, three."

They got Kurt up, one on each side. He regained consciousness for a second and looked at their gloved hands. He furrowed his brow in question but closed his eyes again and let them lead him. Roger scooped up the papers and bag as they headed out the door. Anita closed the door, ensured it was locked, and they stepped out into the cool October air.

33: Roger

October 17, 2017

Kurt stirred as they pulled into the driveway. Anita twisted and looked at Kurt sprawled out in the back seat. He shifted and snored again.

"I'm pleased the extraction went so well. I am eager to get Kurt in and examine him. This will be the last one."

Roger gave her a sideways glance. *I hope you're right.*

He parked the car near the side door and cut the engine. "Give me a second to open the door and turn the lights on," he said sternly. He knew that when she got excited, she acted like a four-year-old.

He got out and looked to ensure he was close enough for the bushes to shield them. The last thing they needed was to draw any attention to themselves. Once Roger opened the door, he walked through the kitchen into the makeshift lab. He flicked the overhead fixture, and it lit up the room with a washer, dryer, folding counter, desk, and a cot they used as a bed. He decided the room was in order and went back to the car.

"This is going to be more difficult. Kurt helped get himself into the car by crawling, but now he's unconscious," Roger said as he surveyed the situation.

"And if he wakes," Anita added, "he will realize we are not at the hospital and may resist. I don't know if I have the strength to fight him." The excitement was gone from Anita's voice.

It took them five minutes to get Kurt out of the car as Anita pulled his legs, and Roger pushed Kurt's back. After that, they worked silently except for Kurt's occasional grunts and moans. *The whole scene would've been comical if it weren't a life-and-death situation.*

One last push/pull, and Kurt teetered on the edge of the seat with his feet on the ground. Anita grabbed both arms while Roger scurried to the other side. He wedged his butt against the door and grabbed Kurt's right arm. Anita wrapped her arm around his left. Finally, Kurt was free, and they hurried through the kitchen to the laundry room. They dropped him onto the cot face first. Roger ran back to close and lock the car door. When he returned, Anita stood over the body. Roger noted her shortness of breath.

She didn't turn to face him. "We've moved sick people before, so why the hell was that so difficult?"

"You're sicker," Roger mumbled.

"What?" she snapped.

Roger ignored her question as he walked to the bed. "Help me flip him over, and then you can get to work."

"Don't be short with me," she snapped back again.

Roger softened his tone. "The quicker you get to work, the better you will feel. That is all I am saying."

They flipped Kurt onto his back, and he coughed. Roger knelt on the bed and looked at Anita. "Restrain him, or not?"

"Just to be sure, use the restraints." She opened a locked cabinet over the desk, took a vial and syringe out, and placed them on the desk.

Kurt woke while Roger tried to place his second wrist into the metal restraint. Kurt looked down at his arms, then at Roger. His eyes grew wide, and he batted Roger with his free arm. He tried to sit up, but Roger successfully secured the free wrist. After that, both legs were free. Kurt scissor-kicked in the air and thrashed on the bed.

Anita tried to grab a leg or a foot, but they moved so fast she couldn't get a hold of them. She bent over further to catch his leg when Kurt kicked her in the stomach, and she flew backward. Roger grabbed the loose arm and clamped the cuff around the wrist. Kurt tried desperately to get free and moved the wheeled bed around the corner of the room. Roger reached down, jammed the wheel lock, and took a deep breath.

"Help!" Anita cried.

Roger looked at Anita in the opposite corner of the room. She looked crumpled, defeated, and tired.

"Help me get up!" she demanded. Tears ran down her face, and blood dropped out of her nose.

Roger crawled over to her and wiped the tears off her cheek. He wrapped his arm around her and helped her stand. She steadied herself, walked over to the desk, opened the cabinet above the desk, and grabbed a different vial. She filled the syringe, tapped it with her finger, and ensured a steady liquid flow.

She turned to Roger, "Fucking hold him down!" she yelled.

Roger grabbed Kurt's two feet and fastened them in place. Anita looked down at the wide-eyed patient and punched Kurt in the stomach. "Asshole," she said.

She stabbed Kurt's arm with the entire length of the syringe needle. Kurt made one more attempt to kick out of the grip. Then his whole body went limp.

"Asshole," she repeated, then walked out of the room. Roger followed her into the living room, where she settled into her wing chair.

"I have to rest before doing the exam. That fight took a lot out of me," Anita said calmly.

"Would you like some tea?" Roger asked.

"No, I just want to sit here and rest." She closed her eyes. "I feel so weak. I don't know if I can even do the examination." She continued talking, and Roger sat on the sofa to listen.

"That was the first experiment that fought back," she added absently. "He is burning up with fever. I have calculated the timeline, and the virus in him is acting differently than it did with others. Or with me."

Roger watched as she rubbed her face on the wing of the chair. He cringed when he saw the spot of red she had left behind.

"What was different? I retraced every step I took with this last experiment."

You mean Cherry. A rush of anger came over Roger. He wanted to reach out and strangle Anita.

"I tweaked my formula after the first two died. And the third died before completing the regimen." She turned her head and wiped the other side of her face on the opposite wing. "Now, the fourth is exhibiting wild, violent tendencies. Just like Mother."

The mention of their mother changed Roger's anger to sadness. He'd been so young when she died, and then he jumped to the fact that Anita had kept him safe all those nights. Guilt pinged in his belly because he wanted Anita to die. His mind drifted to that awful night but stopped. He couldn't let himself be distracted by the past.

"I am scared, Roger." She looked over at him. "I feel the urge to be violent too. The reactions to the antidotes are going the wrong way. I'm going the wrong way. It makes me feel like I am out of control. It makes me feel like I am no better than Mama in her last days."

Tears rolled down her cheeks. Anita wiped them away, stood, and headed to the lab. “I need an answer.”

34: Roger

October 18, 2017

When Roger returned from his early morning drive, Anita sat at the laundry desk. He'd left to clear his mind. The violence Anita showed during the last few experiments troubled him. From his point of view, the virus had stalled, and he feared she wouldn't get any better or worse but just stay in this half-nuts state. The thought made him shiver.

Anita looked engrossed in the data. She muttered to herself as she flipped back and forth through her medical journals. She was close to an answer. He could feel it. But was this a good thing? Did he want her to find a cure? Secretly, it had been about his needs, so the means to the end didn't matter. Did he really want her to die or just go away?

Anita abruptly said, "I can't understand the connection." This was Anita's way of acknowledging his presence, but she didn't turn to look at him.

"What connection?" he asked. He moved further into the room and leaned up against the wall. He looked at Kurt strapped to the bed with some pity. *Poor sucker.*

"The connection between Kurt's reaction and Kurt himself. If I figure that out, I think I'll have the key to the cure." She continued to flip through the pages of her notes.

"Maybe there was something he ate afterward that changed the whole thing. Or there could be something in his blood. Maybe it is his place of origin. There are so many variables. I can't get any answers I need with him in this condition." Anita waved a hand in the general direction of the body. "Though, at this point, I don't know if he would be an active participant even if I didn't over-medicate him." She frowned. "I made a mistake. I shouldn't have let my emotions get the best of me." She swiveled in the chair to face Roger.

Roger moved to stand next to her at the desk. It was painful to watch his sister in such a state of confusion. She had always been so decisive. He laid a hand on her shoulder to comfort her. "Maybe the link is not physical. Maybe it is mental or emotional," he said half-heartedly.

She scrunched up her face. "What the hell are you talking about?"

The dramatic swing in her demeanor took Roger aback. A symptom of the disease he still hadn't gotten used to. He tried to explain his comment. "You know, like *The Grinch Who Stole Christmas*. He didn't know how to be nice and loved until he experienced it in Whoville. And then it all changed. He got a new perspective on things."

Anita shrugged off Roger's hand and stared at him through squinted eyes. Roger shivered. Her eyes were bright pink with conjunctivitis. She didn't even look like the sister he loved. Instead, she looked more like their mother on her last day. He took a step back.

Anita didn't address his explanation. Instead, she hissed, "Where the hell did you go when you were out?"

"Nowhere in particular, just driving around." Her expression made him feel like he shouldn't have suggested anything about the mental or emotional differences between Kurt and her. He knew well how the virus affects the body and the mind. *So why are you only focusing on the physical symptoms?*

"You think *he* is the Grinch?" She pointed to Kurt.

Roger was shocked by her denial of the obvious. He blurted out, "No, just the opposite. I think he is different because he is loved." As soon as the words came out of his mouth, he regretted them. He took two more steps back and prepared for Anita to charge him as their mother had done to their father.

She stood up with both hands in fists. "Are you implying that I am not loved or can't love?" She spoke more through her nose than through her clenched teeth.

Roger took another step back. Over the last few weeks, he had hidden weapons around the house, confident that he could fend off out-of-control sick people, mainly his sister. He backed up another step until he could reach a knife tucked into a stack of towels on a shelf outside the room.

She stared at him. Her rage was in full bloom as blood dripped from her nose. *Wounded bulls looked more inviting than Anita right now.* But rather than charging Roger, she walked to the bed and punched Kurt. He jerked around on the mattress, still attached to restraints. She beat and scratched at him like she was trying to rip off his skin.

Roger rushed over to save Kurt before she killed him. He held her from behind, and she thrashed like a feral cat. Roger let her fight the embrace until he felt her body go slack. When she was tired, he sat her on the chair and went to see if Kurt was still alive. There was a pulse, though it was weak.

"Is he still alive?" she asked. Her voice slurred like a drunk.

"Yes, barely," he said. He ensured his tone was even so as not to trigger another wave of rage.

"Get rid of him. He is useless to me," Anita said and left the room.

Roger watched her leave, then turned back to the experiment. Kurt was supposed to be the last one, and now she'd discarded him like yesterday's trash. Roger didn't know how much more he could take; he needed to be in control of the situation. The latest formula of the vaccine still sat on the desk.

Roger paced. *Should I or shouldn't I give Kurt the prescribed dose?* Of course, if Anita found out, she would take her rage out on him. But if he did it and it worked, Anita would have the cure. He would be free. So, in the end, Roger saw the situation as a win-win.

He locked the door just in case she walked back in and grabbed the vaccine and the syringe. *How much to give him?* Roger turned to the desk and thumbed the open journal for the answer. But the more he read, the more his concern grew. Over the last two weeks, Anita's handwriting had become almost illegible.

Roger sat down to concentrate on the scribbled notes. As he scanned the pages of the journals, he noticed Anita's dosing was all over the place. No wonder she didn't get consistent results. *Why would she do that? She was a brilliant researcher. Had the disease destroyed her mind so much that she couldn't keep track of a baseline?*

Another thought washed over him, something darker and more sinister. *Maybe she was all over the map with dosing because she wasn't looking for a cure anymore. Perhaps she enjoyed herself too much as she tortured and killed people. Maybe this was her way of keeping him close so he didn't leave her.*

Once the thought formed, he couldn't take it back. He hated the idea that she double-crossed him and resented her even more. *So why the hell did he even follow her? Why hadn't he gone his own way when they'd stepped on American soil?*

This whole thing needed to stop, and he would stop it. He decided on a dose, filled the syringe, and administered it to Kurt. Next, he had to get the body from the laundry room to the garage.

Kurt would be safe there until Roger could devise a better plan. He pocketed the vial and checked for more in the little cabinet. He didn't see any, but he grabbed more syringes and closed the door. *Hopefully, Anita will overlook the missing items.*

Roger set up his makeshift dolly beside the bed and eased Kurt onto it. Anita had done a number on his chest, so Roger was careful not to touch those already clotted wounds. Once Kurt was on the dolly, Roger placed a clean blanket on top of him and secured the straps.

He unlocked the door and rolled Kurt into the kitchen. Roger paused momentarily and listened for movement from Anita. He heard nothing. He continued to the side door and out into the stagnant air, then closed the house door. *Was there anyone on the street? No.* He opened the garage door and went to the back corner of the space.

Roger created a little bed nest with an old blanket and sheets, then placed Kurt on top. He covered Kurt and put a water bottle beside him in case he woke up. Roger would check on him in the morning. Hopefully, he will have a plan by then. He locked the garage door and walked back into the house.

Part 3

Professor Belo's journal Entry:

Journal Entry: October 19, 2017

Scope–Continued monitoring of the progress of Marburg Hemorrhagic Fever.

Identification–Patient Alpha 1

Appraisal–New physical attributes–Bleeding from mouth and nose.

New behaviors–Aggression and delirium.

Patient Alpha 1 notes–Too weak to work.

Continued Symptoms–Overall, not feeling well, muscle pain, rash & skin lesions, sore throat & difficulty swallowing, loss of appetite, stomach pains, nausea & vomiting, diarrhea, and conjunctivitis.

Analysis–Patient Alpha 1 exhibits the full spectrum of known symptoms and has entered into the second stage, the last of the disease.

Report–Patient Alpha 1's ability to combat physical symptoms is absent, and the subject slips out of coherency. She can no longer be an unbiased participant in this clinical study. In conclusion, she will start convulsions and fall into a coma before succumbing to the Marburg Hemorrhagic Fever within the next four days.

35: Anita

October 19, 2017–12:00 p.m.

Anita woke up with a killer drama hangover. Her whole body hurt, and her mouth was dry. On her back, she looked up at the thatched fabric she had applied to the ceiling. *I wish I were back in Angola.* She rolled to her side to avoid the thought as it hung in the air beside her bed. It surprised her she yearned for Angola. It wasn't a place where dreams were made.

She didn't belong in Charlotte. But she never felt like she'd belonged anywhere. Tears welled in her eyes, and she wiped them away with the back of her hand. When she looked, she saw blood. She grabbed a tissue and plugged her nostril. *A bloody nose wasn't a good way to start the day.*

Yesterday was crazy.

Anita's stomach turned as she replayed her assault on the experiment. Why did she let herself get to that point? She acted no better than her mother had on the night she died. The one thing Anita had vowed not to do was to lose control. Her theory had been the craziness that engulfed her mother could be controlled.

She had turned on Roger, too. That didn't make her happy, and a wave of anxiety washed over her. *Was she going to kill Roger like her mother had killed her father?*

She tried to change her focus away from the rush of emotions.

Instead, she tried to imagine life after she found the cure. She wanted a cottage with a small yard where she could plant pretty flowers. She would have enough time and money to tend to a garden. She would give fabulous dinner parties in the garden, and everyone would have a grand time. And she could get a puppy. She'd always wanted a dog, but Roger had always refused. He said he wouldn't have a mangy mutt in his house.

Anita groaned when she realized her ideal future didn't include Roger. *Why was that?* It had been the two of them for so long. And yet, he had slipped from her mind. She knew Roger wasn't happy in Charlotte either, yet she had always assumed he would follow her no matter where she went.

But no. It was only fitting that Roger left her in the future. It wasn't as if he would be turning his back on her. They wouldn't need each other anymore. She smiled at the thought. Roger would finally become the powerful man she always knew he could be. A man she helped create.

She finally felt strong enough to get up. Anita rationalized that last night was like an awful thunderstorm, bringing a fresh, cloudless morning the next day. With her bed made, she did a brief stretch, like cats do after a nap. Even though her nose continued to bleed, she felt pretty good.

You are lying to yourself, Anita. Your whole body aches and the pain in your stomach is more intense than it was yesterday.

She went to the window, opened the shades, and let the sunlight come in to chase the cobwebs away. At the window, she let the rays warm her face before she stared down at where the hedge used to be. *Really, I don't give a shit about that hedge. Soon, I will move away.*

Anita eased into her clothes and headed downstairs. There was work to be done, but time ran short. She heated the tea kettle in the kitchen and poured herself a cup of chamomile tea. She carried it into the laundry room. At the door, she stopped. She couldn't remember if Kurt was still in there. She tried to replay the night in her head but got distracted.

Where was Roger?

Typically, he left for coffee and was back by now. Did he leave this morning? Or was he still here? She didn't recall his car parked outside. Frustrated with her memory lapses, she shook her head and tried to refocus.

Anita's head jumped to a horrible notion; maybe she had already found the cure and had forgotten it. It would be like living in the movie *Groundhog Day. Why would she think that?* What a mean trick that would be. She rushed to unlock the laundry room door. The door opened, but the room was empty.

The smell of blood knocked her back against the door and made her cry. It was the last smell she remembered of her mother. Now she realized why she always insisted Roger do the clean-up. She couldn't function with that smell in her head. *Why hadn't he sanitized the room?*

Anita quickly undressed the bloody sheets, shoved them into the washing machine, and started it. She sprayed the mattress with a heavy dose of Lysol, showering a fine mist in the air and floor. She gagged and tried to cover her nose and mouth with the sleeve of her shirt.

Damn it! She rushed out of the room to puke in the kitchen sink. She rinsed the sink but remained bent over while she willed herself not to heave again and tried to force down the anxiety as it gripped her whole body. Anita practiced meditative breathing, closed her eyes, and waited for the moment to pass.

Five minutes later, she calmed down and was ready to face the laundry room again. She paused at the door. There was a palatable bad vibe she had never noticed before. She swallowed hard, forced down the reflux in her throat, and entered the room. It was a nice clear day, and she decided to open a window and get some fresh air, but then she stopped. *But what if the neighbors could smell the blood?* Anita waited until the sheets were ready for the dryer. The dryer was an excellent way to mask smells.

Her mind shifted again to her medical journals, open on the desk. *Had she left them there?* She had never been so sloppy in the past. Another rush of panic came over her. *What if Roger had looked at them? And what if he had? Did he pick up on the lack of connection from one experiment to the next?*

Her hands got cold, and her mouth felt dry again. Had she shown her hand and didn't even know it? She rushed into the kitchen to find her purse and get her phone. Her hands shook as she dialed Roger's number. *Please pick it up. Please pick it up.*

Roger picked up after the third ring. "Just waking up? How are you feeling?" he asked. His voice was peppy.

"Confused," she said, her voice only a whisper.

"Yes, well, a bit of drama played out yesterday," Roger said in a Mr. Clever tone.

"Did I hurt you?" she asked.

"No, no, you didn't hurt me. Besides, I can take it." He continued without letting her speak. "Listen, Anita. I have to go. There is a meeting I need to get to; I will see you a little later." And he disconnected.

Anita felt her nose gush, held the tissue tight and hoped the bleeding would stop. Nosebleeds were one of the less annoying symptoms of her disease. The sudden bouts of uncontrollable anger felt much worse. The symptoms were getting more intense and made her restless. In the end, the anger would become dangerous. Time ran short.

Anita couldn't look at the notes from her experiments anymore. She needed to burn off some anxiety. Anita hated being cooped up. *Maybe a walk?* But then, she thought twice about it. She hadn't walked in the neighborhood for the past ten years. Doing so now would only draw attention. Plus, she wasn't sure she could stabilize her nosebleed or how long it would last. So, she paced like a caged animal through her house.

The buzzer on the washer interrupted her pacing. Anita switched the wet sheets from the washer to the dryer, dispensed three dryer sheets, and set the machine on high for an hour. Then, she opened the small window next to the dryer and let in October's fresh air, which helped her calm her mood.

She took her place at the desk and read the last journal entry. *When did I write this? It doesn't matter. Start from the beginning.* She charted all the variables, looking for when the wrong turn had happened. Anita worked diligently for an hour until the sheets were dry and redressed the bed. She kept the dryer running with only the dryer sheets to cover the smell of death in the air.

Back at the desk, she continued her review. After several hours, she felt good about her progress and wanted to share it with Roger. *Where was Roger?* It was late, and he was usually home by now. She picked up her phone and dialed his number.

While she waited, she stood by the window and looked out over the stump between the neighbor's yard and their own. The whole side yard was a mess, and that giant tree stump mocked them. The neighbors didn't care. How dare they ignore the stress Anita and Roger were under.

The phone interrupted her mental rant about the neighbors. "Anita, I don't think I am coming home tonight." Roger sounded distant and in a rush.

She turned away from the window. "What did you say?"

"I am not coming home tonight. I need some time to think." His voice was sharp.

"Come home, and we can talk about it."

"No."

"You don't have to be snippy. I know I hurt you last night, and I'm sorry. Please don't leave me!" Panic rose in her throat. Without Roger, she was concerned she would lose control, just like Mama.

There was silence before Roger answered. "You didn't hurt me. I felt scared. I am not sure I can trust you anymore," he said.

Anita's voice climbed to a high pitch. "Roger! You know I'm sick, and I'm just not myself. What if the neighbors come over? I can't handle them myself!" Anita hoped the question would cause Roger to reconsider.

There was another silence before he responded. "Anita, you will be fine for one night. Maybe I can find some more lab rats for you." Another pause. "See you in the morning." Before Anita could respond, he hung up.

Anita stared at the phone, then threw it against the wall. "Damn it!" she screamed. "This is unacceptable. It's all unacceptable!" It felt like she was on the brink of uncontrollable rage. The disease was worse. She thought about calling Roger back, to plead her case, but it would do no good. Roger was in one of his moods and had probably already turned his phone off.

Outside the window, she heard Bailey call her dog. "Come on, Alex, let's go for a walk."

The idea infuriated Anita. *If I can't walk, neither can you. Bailey, with her sickly-sweet voice.* The disease made Anita want to rush out of the house and knock that bitch down. But that would almost certainly draw attention. She took a deep breath and tried to regain control. She wanted to confront Bailey, but it had to be away from the prying eyes of neighbors.

Anita moved from the laundry to the living room for a better view. From behind her heavy curtains, she watched Bailey and Alex walk down their front steps, cross in front of Anita's house, and continue down the road. She knew it would be about ten minutes before they returned unless they went around the block. She hated that she knew the neighbor's routine, but now it came in handy.

"I am going to get you, you little bitch." She sounded like the Wicked Witch of the West. It surprised Anita, but the thought of confronting Bailey delighted her heart. Finally, she would get her way in this whole "dead tree" drama. *Bailey wouldn't even know what hit her.* Anita's heart beat fast. She picked up her phone, shoved it in her pocket, and headed out the door.

Anita lingered at the end of the street as she watched both directions for signs of Bailey and Alex. She didn't want to stick out like a sore thumb, so she pulled out her broken phone and pretended to search for something on it, then pretended to call someone. A pang of regret washed over her as she realized she had no one to call. The thought fueled another rush of rage. Bailey and Alex turned the corner and walked toward her. *The feud stops today.*

36: Bailey

2:00 p.m.

As soon as Bailey turned the corner, she saw Anita a block away. Bailey's stomach turned. The last thing she wanted was another confrontation with the neighbor. The truce had done nothing to ease the tension between the two households.

Bailey prided herself on being likable. But with little effort, Jordan and Bailey became archenemies between Roger and Anita. Bailey knew they were pissed off over that damn tree. Tension had resulted from not giving in to their unrealistic demands. The tree was dead and gone. *What's the problem now?*

Bailey watched Anita march up the sidewalk towards her and stopped abruptly in Bailey's path. "I want to talk to you about the hedge." Anita's hands were on her hips. The stance had become an almost iconic pose for Anita over the last month.

Bailey tried to maintain a blank expression while she weighed her options. How was she going to get around Anita? One option was to run into oncoming traffic. As dangerous as it was, it was still viable. The other option was to skirt around her on the upside of the slope, but she might trip on Alex's leash. Alex barked at Anita. *Does Alex sense my anxiety?*

"Did you hear me? I want to discuss the hedge!" Anita yelled over the drone of the cars as they passed by.

"I heard you, Anita. But one, I'm done talking because there is nothing more to discuss. And two, you standing there yelling at me isn't my idea of a discussion. What part of 'leave us alone' don't you understand?" Bailey and Alex took a step forward, and Anita stepped back.

"Keep your dog away from me!" Anita commanded with a tongue click.

So much attitude.

"Get out of my way, Anita."

Bailey took another step forward, avoided Anita's gaze, and choked up on the leash. Bailey charged through Anita's invisible barricade, walked down the driveway, and let herself into the backyard without a second glance. But Anita followed on her heels and pushed through the gate as Bailey unleashed Alex.

"What are you doing about the hedge?" she demanded.

Luckily, rabbit poop distracted Alex, and he was off in search of fresh droppings. Bailey turned and found herself face-to-face with an extremely pissed-off woman. *Shit. Now, what was she supposed to do?* She needed to get Anita back to the other side of the gate.

"Listen, Anita. I didn't invite you into my backyard, and I want you to leave." Bailey pointed to the gate.

Anita stood there like a stubborn bull. "Which is it? Fix the hedge, build a fence, or plant something? I can't tell you how much sleep we have lost over this thing. What are you going to do about it?"

This was the breaking point for Bailey. Her nerves frayed; she'd had enough. "You? You are losing sleep over this? Screw you. Like this has been a walk in the park for us. We can't even leave the house without you or Roger verbally assaulting us! You are both bat crap crazy!"

Anita tried to interrupt, but Bailey continued. "Don't even

think about trying to butt in as I'm speaking. I have listened to you yell at us like we created the situation just to piss you off. But, contrary to what you seem to think, we have better things to do. On the top of that list is trying to clean and pick up the pieces after the tree came down."

Bailey took a deep breath and continued. "It was a damn 75-year-old tree! We have lived here for ten years! We have tried to do everything to accommodate your concerns about the tree. Even up to the day it came down! As soon as we confirmed it was dead, we did the responsible thing and had it removed. Yet, despite that, you'll still not satisfied. You want more!"

Bailey's voice stayed even. "We won't do jack shit to the hedge because we have no more money. You seem to forget that Roger and you rescinded your offer to pay half the removal cost the day before, so we had to pay the entire amount. Plus, we live in an Enterprise Zone." Bailey let the last sentence hang in the air. She wasn't sure she should have said it.

"What the hell does that mean?" Anita's face got redder.

Bailey shot back, "What it means is they can develop the land for commercial use even though it is currently residential. As a matter of fact, Jordan and I have sold to the state, and I heard rumors they will develop the land for a state trooper's outpost. I mean, why not? The land is close to the two highway interchanges and with all the development across the street...." Bailey stopped her tirade. *Why the hell am I trying to explain this to this nut job?* She raised her arm and pointed to the gate again. "Just! Get! Out! Anita!"

The response Bailey got was like every other from these neighbors. Anita ignored her. Bailey had said what she needed to say. She turned and walked away. Two ways to deal with bullies are to stand up for yourself or ignore them. Bailey did both.

Over her shoulder, Bailey could hear Anita ask again, "What

are you going to do with the hedge?"

Lost in her own rage, Bailey didn't see Anita as she moved toward her. She clicked back into the present just before Anita put her hand on Bailey's shoulder. Anita tried to swing Bailey around with her right hand, but Bailey resisted. She dug in her heel, formed a fist, and swung. With an upward thrust, she caught Anita on the chin. The punch knocked Anita back a couple of feet, and she lost her balance.

Bailey's goal was to get away, not stay and fight. Anita was taller and outweighed her by at least fifty pounds. *Not to mention she is crazy.* Bailey turned, and Anita jumped on her back. *Yep, she outweighs me!*

Bailey fell to her knees and rolled to the right as Anita's hands tightened around her neck. Bailey reached around and shoved her thumbs into Anita's eyes. It was like a magic button. Anita screamed and released her hold. Bailey scrambled to get up and ran to the potting shed.

Bailey's mind raced. *Is this a psychotic break?* It wasn't just an argument between neighbors anymore. It was a complete break from reality. Bailey understood the concept, but this was her first time having witnessed one. It was a completely different story.

As blood seeped from her nose and mouth, Anita charged Bailey. She caught Bailey by the shoulder and shoved her into the raised planter full of lavender. Bailey whirled around as Anita lunged for her neck again. Bailey sidestepped, which avoided the death grip, but was trapped in a corner. She felt like the bunnies Alex hunted.

Anita grabbed Bailey by the shoulders and pinned her against the potting shed. Anita's eyes blazed, and it scared Bailey. *She is going to kill me. Kill me over a tree and a fence. She's crazy!*

The lapse in concentration proved to be Bailey's last mistake. Anita moved in for the kill. She grabbed Bailey by the front of her shirt, picked her up, and shoved her through the plate-glass window on the side of the shed. Shards of glass flew everywhere. Bailey landed on her back, and everything went black.

37: Roger

3:00 p.m.

Roger was cautious as he walked down the sidewalk beside the neighbor's backyard. He had the good sense to park on the next street and sneak into the gate with no one raising an eyebrow, namely Helen, from across the street.

At the gate, he took a deep breath and let it out. He hoped that was enough to prepare him for the scene that awaited him. Anita had called in a panic, much like all her waking moments lately, but this time, it was different. She had attacked Bailey, and she didn't know what to do. She'd said, "Bailey is unconscious! There is blood everywhere! And that damn dog keeps barking!"

And so, Roger had let last night's drama go and came to Anita's side, brown bag in hand.

Roger had grabbed a wire cutter and a ham bone from the university's kitchen before he left. He hoped the bone would distract the dog while he breached the wire fence between the backyards. Hopefully, it would only take a couple of snips. He didn't have to be careful, just quick.

Roger looked down at his suit and smoothed the front of the jacket. There was no time to change. Thus, one more outfit he would ruin with manual labor. *I am so done with Anita's bullshit.* He took another breath, opened the gate, and slipped in the door. He shook the bone out of the bag and kicked it toward the dog as he charged him. Alex grabbed the bone and hurried to the yard's far corner. *Good, just as planned.*

"Roger, back here!" she yelled in a high-pitched squeal.

He turned the corner and saw Anita draped over the raised plant bed. As he moved closer, she pointed to the shed. "She's in there."

He opened the door to the shed and knelt beside Bailey. There was so much glass but little blood. *Thank God for small favors.* He checked for a pulse and was relieved to find one. "Anita, come here and help me."

"I'm too tired to help," she whined.

He jumped up. "No! This is your mess. Help clean it up!"

She huffed as she stood up and pushed herself off the ledge of the raised planter. At Roger's side, she whispered, "I didn't mean to."

Roger ignored her comment. There was no time to coddle her and her childlike behavior. "Take the wire cutter and find a place along the fence we can fit through."

"What?"

Roger stood up and got close to her face. He spoke through gritted teeth. "Find a sparse spot in the hedge and start cutting the wire fence so we can bend it back and slip through."

She didn't move. Instead, she stared at the tool in her hand.

"Now!" He turned back to Bailey before Anita could protest.

It took him several minutes to move the glass away from Bailey's body. The shed was too small for him to get ahold of her to carry, so he grabbed her wrists and dragged her out onto the grass. He looked to see what Alex was doing. Roger was relieved to see the dog hunkered down in a hole, focused on the newfound bone. *Move quickly. You don't know how long that will last.*

Anita trotted back to Roger. “I think I made the hole big enough to get through.” She bent over and panted.

Roger wanted to reach out and pick up some of the plant debris she had collected in her hair during her efforts. *Later. It doesn’t matter what she looks like.* “I can’t do a deadlift, so we must drag her. Get the right side.”

Anita did what she was told, and they went to the fence. “Go through the hole first.” He pointed. “Then I will come through, and we will drag her together. Once she is in our yard, go inside and get your shit together.” He eyed Anita as she opened her mouth to protest but said nothing.

Roger had the left arm and Anita the right. “On three, pull. One, two, three.”

Bailey’s shirt and pants snagged on the ground cover and made the process difficult. They ran through the process three times before all three were through the hole.

“It’s like birthing a child.” Anita giggled.

Roger stopped and dropped Bailey’s arm. “No, Anita. It isn’t. Not by a long shot.” He pointed to their house. “Inside. Now!”

Roger unlocked the garage and opened the door wide enough to grab the dolly. He heard Kurt moan. Shit, not now. *Go back to sleep.*

He mumbled to himself as he rolled Bailey into the cart. “One minute, she is trying to kill the neighbor, and the next, she is making jokes. This is ridiculous. And I have to go behind her and clean up her mess.” He stopped and looked down at the front of his suit. “And I’m the only one left dirty.”

Once Bailey was in the cart, Roger bent the fence back into place, so it looked like nothing had happened. At the garage, he opened the door and dumped Bailey in the middle of the room. Kurt moaned again, and Roger checked his watch. Kurt needed another dose. *What am I going to do about Bailey?*

#

Roger stood in the doorway to the living room and watched Anita. Her head was back against the side of the wingback chair, her eyes closed. Caught pieces of lavender, sage, and bushes poked from her scalp, but she didn't seem to care. She looked tired and defeated. *The disease had taken her mind and robbed her of the typical high-level energy. She was only a shell of her former self.*

Roger knelt beside her and tended to her scratches and bruises in silence. She put her hand on Roger's cheek and stroked it as she fell asleep. He could sense the change in Anita's resolve and was surprised he was still concerned. She was close to death. But he didn't want to think about it at the moment. Instead, he used a cotton square moistened with hydrogen peroxide to clean her scratches. *These wounds won't heal. Her body's defenses are too busy fighting the fever.*

As Anita slipped deeper into sleep, her body relaxed, and Roger knew it was safe to step away. He stood and quietly backed into the kitchen, careful not to disturb the sleeping beast.

Has she really come to the end? He rested his butt against the edge of the sink. *Would it soon be over, and he would be free?* The thought both excited and scared him. Now, he would get his life back. Or lose it all. He reached for the bottle of vodka. "This calls for a toast. A martini would be nice," he said out loud.

He heard Anita stir in the living room as he touched the bottle. He withdrew his hand. It may be a little early for a celebration. The image of him and Anita in the closet on the night of their mother's life flashed in his head. The memory always conjured up emotions of sadness and anger in him, and he was tired of the internal conflict. He walked to the living room and stared at Anita. *She looks peaceful while she sleeps.*

He knew the disease had taken its toll on her, but they were in no position to quit now. Not with Kurt and the neighbor in the garage. Somewhere in his own brain, he knew Anita had crossed a line. The use of strangers was one thing, but a neighbor? *The situation had gotten out of control.*

38: Roger

4:00 p.m.

Anita stirred again, and Roger knew she would wake soon. *Hopefully, more coherent.* He turned and walked into the kitchen to make some tea. While he filled the kettle, he gazed through the window over the backyard and the garage.

"What the hell are we going to do with the neighbor?" he said aloud.

"We will use her as a lab rat, and if the experiment doesn't work, we will kill her!" Anita screamed from the kitchen doorway. Her voice surprised Roger, and he dropped the kettle into the sink. It smashed a glass and sent shards onto the countertops.

"Shit, you scared me. I thought you were sleeping." Roger was fixated on the broken glass as he spoke. It was one of his beloved martini glasses. His first response was to feel sad; it was just another thing taken away from him by his sister. But then the feeling turned to resentment.

Roger picked up the pieces one by one and placed them in a plastic bag. He paused and examined one dagger-like piece. *Could I kill her with it?*

"Roger, are you listening to me?"

He turned just enough to acknowledge and view her from the

corner of his eye. Anita was in her quintessential pose, hands on hips as she stood in the doorway. Her face was pure evil, with pursed lips, flared nostrils, and narrowed eyebrows. *She had rested. And now she was ready for blood.*

He laid down the glass shard, picked up the kettle, and continued to fill it with water. "Let me make you a cup of tea to calm you down." Roger turned on the gas burner. Click, click, poof. He adjusted the flame and set the kettle down. *If only it were that easy to control Anita's mood.*

"I don't want a goddamn cup of tea! I want to find a cure and get the hell out of here! I want to go to the garage and pluck that smile off that bitch's face! I want you to be more supportive!"

She continued to rant about her needs, but Roger had turned and tuned out. *More supportive, my ass. I killed for you, bitch!* The anger in his virtual voice drowned out Anita's voice. *Maybe I should tell her what I've been doing all these months.* He shook his head and muttered, "No, not now. It isn't the right time."

"Not the right time for what?" Anita asked. She moved into the kitchen, now inches away from Roger's ear.

He turned to face her and put his palm on her cheek. *I don't know if I should hate, love, thank, or reject you—my silly Anita.* He gazed into her eyes, and for a brief moment, he saw his big sister from childhood. He smiled at those eyes, and the fear of her he hadn't been able to shake for days disappeared.

The kettle whistled, and the tender moment was lost. Anita's eyes narrowed again. The fire was back. Roger side-stepped her and reached for the boiling kettle.

"Yes. I think a cup of tea would be good," Anita said, calmer than she had been a moment before. Her eyes teared up as she continued. "Yes, I am tired and not thinking straight, but this doesn't change my conviction. I still want to find the cure for the Marburg Virus." She slumped down into one of the kitchen chairs. She put her hands on her cheeks and bowed her head. "I am physically weak, so I must depend on you even more."

If I have to carry any more, you will break me! He filled two mugs with chamomile tea and brought them to the table. He sat beside her and placed a mug in front of Anita.

Anita stared at the mug. "You still want to leave Charlotte, right?" she asked. They didn't agree much, but on this point, he was on board, and he would leave this place in a second.

"Yes, more than anything," he said. They sipped tea silently for five minutes, each in their own worlds.

The silence broke when Anita sat up straight and slammed her hands on the table. "We have to finish this thing!"

She attempted to get up, but Roger caught her left arm and pulled her back into her seat. "Hold on there, Anita, we can't charge out there without a plan." He patted her arm. "We need to be strategic about this. Bailey is the first one that anyone will worry about." *That we know of.*

He cleared his throat and let his voice be smooth. "You don't want to be arrested when you are so close, do you? Scientific discoveries mean nothing unless they can be documented and recreated. It isn't the time to go all willy-nilly." Roger let a slight, evil grin cross his face. *Well played, Roger. It sounds like you almost care.*

39: Bailey

3:30 p.m.

Bailey woke up in the dark. The room was dark, except for a crack of daylight near the ceiling. *At least it was light.* She looked away because the light made her dizzy. Bailey closed her eyes and did some physical and mental system checks. She could feel and move her arms, fingers, legs, and feet. *That's good.*

As the fog lifted, Bailey's stomach responded with a sharp pain as her stomach churned; she turned her head and threw up. *Usually, after I throw up, I feel better. But not today.* The episode had made all the systems in her body go into overdrive. She shook like it was 30 below but sweated like she had just run a marathon. Her whole body ached. To distract herself from the pain, she focused on her surroundings.

The smell of mold and dirt suggested she was lying on the ground. Bailey shifted and was quick to sit up. Must and mold were not her friends. The last thing she wanted was to sneeze. She snapped to attention when the room spun. She turned and threw up again. It still didn't relieve her.

Bailey heard a faint moan. *Was that from me? Maybe I am still asleep.* A moment later, she heard it again. *No, that was definitely not me.* A flash of memory, and she remembered the last minutes before everything went black. She had been in the backyard with

Anita and…*that damn tree.*

Bailey's eyes cleared and adjusted to the dim light in the room. She fine-tuned her senses to get a handle on her surroundings. There wasn't much for her to observe. Bailey shook her head at the mental image of Anita, full-bore angry and with giant conjunctivitis eyes.

"That bitch be crazy," she said out loud. Then she heard something move behind her. "Hello?" she called out.

Why did I do that? Because every scary movie starts with some dumb person saying hello. Rookie move, Bailey. She tensed for another attack. *Am I the quarry now?* A chill ran up her spine. And, for the first time, she realized how scared she was. *What was going to happen next?*

Bailey felt around to find something she could use as a weapon, avoiding the two vomit spots. To the left was something cold and hard, with several prongs. *A rake?* She tugged at it, but it resisted. She twisted her butt to face it and pulled it again with both hands. It gave way and bobbed her on the top of her head along with other long-handle tools.

Quiet like a church mouse.

Bailey froze to see if the thing in the corner was disturbed. She held her breath for thirty seconds but didn't hear any movement. *Is it dead, asleep, or getting ready to attack me?*

Rake in her grasp, she tried to regroup. She replayed her last moments of memory, the altercation with Anita on the sidewalk next to the driveway. *Did anyone see or hear it?* She remembered her physical fight in the backyard and instinctively reached up to feel the back of her head. It was wet and matted with dirt and leaves. *Not good, not good at all.*

A wave of panic and nausea overcame her. *Please don't get sick again, please no.* The thought of getting sick was enough actually to make her ill. She could handle blood and gore. But puke, that was another story. *Puppies, think of puppies, Bailey.* The wave passed.

If someone had seen the violent display, they would have at least investigated, maybe even called the police. No cops, so I guess no one saw the attack. Of course, that assumes that she was still in the neighborhood. *Am I still in the neighborhood?*

Another wave of panic. She was injured, and if she had the chance, would she be able to run and get help? Bailey knew damn well she couldn't fight Anita in this condition. Chances were, Roger would be close behind. Not to mention that her eyes had adjusted to the darkness. If the doors opened, she would be blind.

Bailey's mind jumped to another question. Was she being watched right now? She scanned the room and looked for a blinking light or a reflective lens that could be a camera, but she saw nothing. That didn't satisfy her. So where was she? *Had Anita kidnapped her?*

She recalled the conversation she and Jordan had about Anita and Roger's mental stability. She'd described Anita as bat crap crazy. *But was I being snarky, or was she really crazy?*

Of course, confronting a neighbor in their backyard and pushing them through a plate-glass window was pretty crazy. What she wanted to know was whether she would make it out of the situation alive. The question turned her stomach. Bailey choked back the vomit as her gag reflex settled down. Instead, the thing across the room puked. The sound snapped Bailey from her train of thought. *Is this thing going to attack? Or maybe it was being held captive as well.*

Curiosity flooded her brain, and she scrambled on her hands and knees to where the sound came from. She reached up and touched a head of hair. It flailed its arms to shield its body. Human.

"It's okay. I won't hurt you." She added silently *unless you are a zombie, then I am going to beat the living...Bailey, you watch too many bad horror films.*

The person seemed to relax. She put her hand on his face and could feel a weak smile.

"What's your name?" she asked.

"Kurt Hollaway," he said in a sad voice.

Under normal circumstances, Bailey would have said, "Nice to meet you." But that just didn't seem right. So instead, she said, "We're going to get out of this. I promise."

Bailey was shocked to hear the confidence in her voice. *How are you going to do that, Wonder Woman?* The pit at the bottom of her stomach churned, which fueled energy in her brain. Bailey thought of all sorts of questions to ask Kurt, but she held herself back. After all, this was not a research paper she would have done in college. It was a real-life crisis. *Cut to the chase, Bailey.*

Images of all the scary movies she had ever seen flashed in her head, sending shivers down her spine. Were they being watched? She'd checked earlier, but now that she was more alert, she scanned the room again. *Still no evidence of any cameras.*

She leaned close to Kurt's ear and whispered, "Are we being watched?"

Kurt shook his head. "I don't think so."

This information was comforting, but maybe they *were* listening. Bailey leaned forward again. "Let's keep the talking to a minimum and at a whisper, just in case." He nodded.

Still close to his ear, she said, "I have three questions. Do you know who did this to you? Do you know where we are? Can you move on your own when the time comes to make a break for it?"

There was a long pause, and Kurt responded in a harsh, dry voice, "It was Anita Belo. I think we're in a garage or shed. And yes, I think I will be able to move."

Bailey sat back on the ground to ponder the new information. In the eight years she had lived next door, she could count on one hand the number of times she had seen Anita Belo outside. Now,

Anita was out gallivanting around the neighborhood, fighting and kidnapping people in broad daylight.

She wasn't at all surprised she had been kidnapped. She was, it seemed, Anita's nemesis. But to kidnap a stranger seemed like the "crazy" line had been crossed. Bailey had always assumed Anita was a little off-center, but the severity of the situation was evident; Anita was dangerous. If they didn't escape, Anita was going to kill both of them.

Was Roger part of this deadly activity, or was he a victim, too? Maybe it was a case of Stockholm Syndrome. She couldn't be sure, and it wasn't the time to analyze it. So, she played it safe and concluded that they were both evil. Her focus was when the doors opened, and the final battle ensued. She had to accept it would be two against herself and what was left of Kurt. She didn't like the odds.

God, I hate conflict! She didn't always avoid confrontations. She could think of quite a few occasions where she'd stood up and defended herself. *Is this situation any different?*

A jolt of courage made her blood move. And for a moment, she was high on adrenaline. *I am going to kick some crazy bitch ass!* Then, the reality of the situation sank in. Those previous occasions didn't involve life-or-death danger.

Bailey said out loud, "Welcome to the jungle, baby!"

"What?"

She looked in Kurt's direction and said to the darkness, "Never mind."

40: Bailey

4:00 p.m.

Bailey's other senses kicked into high gear, and most of her eyesight was gone from the darkness. She sat and became conscious of the mildew that rose from the floor. The scent made her nostrils burn, and she sneezed. They weren't in a basement. The air was too thick and hot. Plus, she could hear the cicadas' hum in the trees.

Kurt was right. We must be in a shed or garage.

Either way, both had doors that swung out like kitchen cabinets. *The hinges.* Maybe she could loosen the hinges to throw them off their game. In the backyard scuffle with Anita, it had been midday. The light that came through the crack high on the wall was bright. *Is it the same day, or had she been unconscious for over twenty-four hours?* She sniffed her underarms. It wasn't scientific, but she could smell deodorant, so it was most likely the same day.

Bailey could hear traffic. Cars, trucks, and other large vehicles passed regularly. And then she heard the most welcoming sound of them all. Someone made an illegal U-turn, turned, and gunned the engine as they headed for the highway. It was a sound she heard every day, but she had never thought it would bring her to happy tears. *I'm close to home! I must be in Anita's shed or garage.*

She wiped the tears away with the arm of her tee shirt. *We might just get out of this alive.* She looked over at Kurt, who had fallen back to sleep. At least she hoped he was asleep. Kurt let out a little snort as if to say, "Yes, I am still here."

Bailey couldn't guess how long she had been there or how long she had been awake, but she knew it was long enough for the cornucopia of smells to creep into her nose. It made her sneeze and her stomach turn.

She chastised herself for not thinking like MacGyver. *He'd have fashioned a crowbar out of the rake already and be free, Bailey. What do you have?*

She stood up and felt her way around the garage, and mentally cataloged its contents: a hose, a rake, a shovel, and a bag of fertilizer. It wasn't much, but she tried not to be discouraged. Along with the gardening tools, she found an assortment of plastic bins, some cardboard boxes, and a bike. Bailey snorted at the thought of either Anita or Roger on a bike. How often had she seen either of them outside doing anything other than walking to or from the car, micro-managing the hired help, or bitching out her and Jordan?

Focus, Bailey. Your primary goal is to get out alive.

On her inspection of the garage, she located a small crack at the door frame. She pulled up a plastic tub, sat, and peered out. Bailey could see Anita's kitchen door, based on her own cookie-cutter house layout, and knew they used that door most of the time. She assumed this was where they would come from...she hoped.

Her nose was close to the crack, and she could feel the October air outside. Though it was still hot, it was crisp, unlike the stagnant air inside the garage. Bailey sucked in the fresh supply and was comforted. *So close to freedom, I can taste it.*

What the hell was going on? Something big, and she had no clue. *I bet kidnapping her wasn't the craziest thing Anita and Roger had done.* The thought made her shiver. She turned away, let her eyes adjust to the darkness again, and counted how long it took. That amount of time was all she had as an advantage once the door was open.

Less than a minute.

She rearranged the one-car garage with the few items she had found. While she worked, she ran through as many scenarios as she could create. As she did, she paced and took turns being each person in the scene. Bailey felt like she was the director of a play and worked out the staging for the actors, though she had to play all the parts. She reviewed each scenario, best to worst, and then decided which one she liked best. Hopefully, they would play their roles, and it all would play out the way she wanted.

Bailey was convinced Kurt was strong enough to get out by himself, and she had to plan on that reality. She whispered, "I need to hide Kurt when the time comes. He needs to be safe until I can get help."

A cell phone would help right now. Bailey patted her pockets for her phone. *Damn, they took it.* But then she remembered it sat on the table in her home office. *I'm never going to hear the end of that!*

Her head raced and yet was clear at the same time. *If I had a choice and could only attack one of them, would I pick Roger or Anita?* She shuddered at the question. It's like being asked, "Do you want to be shot or stabbed?" She shook her head. "I prefer neither, thank you."

"Prefer what?" Kurt asked. Bailey didn't notice that Kurt had woken up minutes before.

She rushed over to him. "You're awake. How are you feeling?"

"Less like a Mack truck hit me. Maybe more like a Volvo." Then he repeated, "You prefer what?"

Bailey reached out and felt his head as she checked for a fever. "It feels like you don't have a fever anymore. That's a good thing."

Kurt changed the subject. "Anita always comes in first."

"What?" *Was Kurt crazy, too? Is he contagious?* She stood and took a step backward.

"When I woke, you were pacing and muttering to yourself. I assume you are planning an attack. I bet Anita would be the first. Anita is the kind of person who always comes into the room first to make sure everyone sees her. I've seen her push her way through a door just to be first in. It's rude." Kurt propped himself up into a sitting position.

"I guess you *are* feeling better." *That's a good thing. One less thing to worry about.* Bailey continued to pace and mull over her scenes. "It doesn't surprise me about Anita. By the way, how do you know her?"

"Actually, I am feeling better. I was sick for a few weeks, so it feels good not to be so sick. And I know her because she is one of my professors."

"And she kidnapped you, too?"

"Well, that is where my haze starts. I'm not sure how I got here."

Bailey walked over to the back corner of the garage, picked up the water bottle, and handed it to Kurt. "They left you with some water. You should try to drink a little. Then, see if it sits well in your stomach, and drink some more."

Kurt took the bottle and held it up to her. "Do you want some?"

"No, it is all yours. I'm guessing you have been without water for much longer than I have."

"Why are we not whispering anymore?"

"Good question. I had the time to inspect the room. First, the door is locked from the outside. We couldn't be so lucky. We are going to face our attackers." Bailey laughed at her attempt at a joke. "But I didn't find any cameras or listening devices. So, that's a good thing. We can plan and move around without attracting attention. But, on the other hand, the bad news is that there isn't much we can use as weapons or distractions."

"My head is a little clearer now. And my stomach seems to be happy with the water." Kurt took a swig off the bottle. "I think I can help you set up a trap."

"No, I need you to be as still as possible. But you will need to move fast when the time comes. Tell me what happened to get you here if you are up to it."

"I'll try. But before I do, there is one thing you should know." He took another pull from the bottle. "I don't think Anita knows I'm in here."

"What? Are you saying Roger did this all himself?" She shook her head. It didn't add up. "Wait, I'm confused. I always thought Anita was the master of the house."

Kurt sat up a little taller. "She is, but something happened last night. It ended with her thinking I was dead." He shook his head. "It's all surreal. I ended up in here, but I think Roger was supposed to kill me. Instead, he must have decided to save me."

Bailey pulled the plastic tub next to him and sat. "Kurt, you'll have to start from the beginning."

41: Roger

4:15 p.m.

Roger checked his watch. He knew Kurt was about a half an hour past his drug installment. It made him nervous. He didn't know what was going on in the garage. *Was Kurt awake, dying, or worse, recovered?* Kurt had been unconscious when Roger pushed Bailey into the garage. But how long could he go without medicine? Roger damned Anita for going off half-cocked and kidnapping Bailey.

"Why do you continue to check your watch?" Anita's voice raised accusation. "What the hell are you waiting for, a date?"

Roger reached over to place a palm on her arm, but she shrugged it off.

"You're going to run out on me and leave me to clean up this mess!?" Anita waved her arms around and then pointed outside.

"Listen here, Anita, this mess is all your doing," he shot back, stressing the word mess. "The only reason I'm still here is because of my loyalty to you. Do you really think I give a crap about finding a cure and saving those poor suckers in Angola?"

The statement set Anita off. "You said you wanted to leave Charlotte!" Her voice was at full volume.

Roger met her volume and shot back, "I did. I do. But I sure as hell don't want to go back to Africa, and I don't want to go anywhere with you! You are toxic!"

"I'm not toxic. I am *sick*!" she cried.

"You were toxic long before you got sick, bitch!" Roger screamed. He jumped out of the chair and stood at the sink.

Anita grabbed the half-full cup of tea and threw it at him. Roger ducked, but not enough. The cup bounced off the corner of his glasses. The tea soaked his new silk tie as his glasses and cup landed on the floor. *Damn it!*

He bent to pick up his glasses and saw Anita as she charged him. There was fury in her eyes, scarlet and piercing. This time, the anger was directed toward him. He was about to experience firsthand the terror Bailey and all the other experiments must have felt. *She is going to kill me!*

Before he could stand straight, she was on him, her hands around his throat. Roger clawed at them as they tightened. The more he clawed, the tighter the grip. His eyes bulged, and his sight darkened at the edges. On the verge of passing out, he heard faint yelling and screaming. *Was that him having an out-of-body experience?* No, that sound came from outside.

Anita heard it, too. She released her chokehold and rushed to the back door. "I should have finished that bitch off when I had the chance!"

Roger crumpled to the kitchen floor while he tried to catch his breath. He held up one hand. "Anita, wait! Don't go out there! What about all of your work up until now?"

She paused with her hand on the doorknob. "Screw my work. At the most, I have a day left before I die. She's the one who did this to me, and I want that bitch's head on a platter!"

42: Jordan

4:10 p.m.

Jordan headed home from his office at four. He was glad he only worked five minutes from home. The latest deadline loomed over his head. And he went to the office early to work in peace. He hated that the demands of the job conflicted with the need to keep an eye on Bailey. He hated being away from Bailey and Alex. He smiled. Silly as it sounded, he still enjoyed being around his wife even after all these years.

His neck stiffened as he prepared to make the U-turn beside the house. The thought of the mess next door stressed him out. He had been reluctant to leave Bailey alone in the house this morning.

But she had insisted, "Please, go. I will be fine. The sooner you go, the sooner you'll be back. I promise not to do anything stupid while you're gone."

How had this thing with the tree gotten so out of hand? Could they have done something differently? He shook his head. Sometimes, you can't please everyone, no matter how much you try.

After he completed the U-turn, he pulled into the driveway and parked. Jordan put the key in the fence lock but noticed it was already unlocked and muttered, "I told Bailey to keep it locked."

He entered the backyard, where Alex greeted him with a wiggly butt. Jordan fluffed the top of his head. "Hey there, Alex, where is Mama?" The terrier cocked his head and barked at Jordan. He barked again and ran over to a basket that held outside toys.

Jordan smiled. "Okay, let me just put my stuff down inside."

Alex sat down next to the balls and barked again. *Why are you alone in the backyard?* Neither he nor Bailey made a habit of that. After all, Alex was a terrier. When he was unsupervised, it meant an opportunity to get into trouble.

At the back door, Jordan twisted the handle. *Well, at least she kept this door locked.* He turned the key, opened the door, and placed his day bag on the stool inside. When he looked back at Alex, he saw the leash on a lawn chair. *They must have just gotten back from a walk.*

Jordan grabbed two balls from the basket, threw one, and kept the second. Unfortunately, Alex had never learned the concept of "drop it." Alex ran after the ball and caught it. But then he dropped it and picked up something Jordan couldn't identify. Alex trotted to the yard's far corner where the potting shed was, dropped the thing in his mouth, and whimpered.

Jordan followed. *Alex, please tell me you didn't catch a rabbit. I really don't want to clean up that mess.* "What is it, boy? Did Timmy fall down the well again?" He bent down to see what the dog had between his legs and inspected it. *A fresh bone?*

"Where did you get that?"

Alex barked, and it was Jordan's turn to cock his head to one side to question the meaning. Alex growled as he focused on the bone and then on the side of the shed. Jordan got closer and grabbed Alex by the collar. "Come on and leave the bunnies alone."

As the words escaped his mouth, he saw the large plate-glass window on the side of the shed wasn't there anymore. He rushed to the open door of the shed. It was empty, but the floor was covered with shattered glass and blood.

"Bailey? How the hell did you break the window?" Jordan's mind raced. *Maybe she is hurt.*

He rushed to the back door and called Bailey's name but got no response. *Has she passed out?* Jordan ran upstairs into the bathroom and pulled open the shower curtain, expecting to see her in the tub, bleeding to death. But she wasn't there. He picked up the phone to call Helen Platte, the across-the-street neighbor. *Maybe she went there to get help.* The phone rang until the answering machine picked up. Jordan disconnected.

"Damn it!"

He called Bailey's cell. As it rang, he could hear an echo of it in Bailey's office. *She left the phone behind again.*

Panic made Jordan's head pound. "Where the hell are you?" *Maybe Helen took Bailey to the hospital.*

Jordan returned downstairs, called Alex in, grabbed his keys and phone, and made a beeline to the Platte's.

"I shouldn't have left Bailey alone. Fuck my deadline!" Jordan said as he jogged across his front lawn and passed Helen's car to the front stoop of the Platte's. He banged on the door desperately, and his mind raced while he waited. *Was Bailey in danger?* His blood pumped, and his anxiety was high. His whole body shook, and he jumped on the stoop to expel his nervous energy.

Mr. Platte answered the door, "Oh hey Jordan, what's up?"

Helen's husband was in his 80s, and nothing seemed to excite him anymore. At the moment, his calm Southern demeanor irritated Jordan. There was no time for neighborly pleasantries. "Is Bailey with you and Helen?" Jordan said through clenched teeth.

Mr. Platte acknowledged Jordan's edginess with a frown but didn't answer Jordan's question. Instead, he turned to yell into the house, "Helen, have you seen Bailey?"

Deep in the house, a muffled voice yelled, "No, I haven't seen her for a couple of days now." Helen's voice got closer. By the time she was at the end of the sentence, she was at her husband's side. "What's wrong? Do you want to come inside?"

"No!" Jordan snapped. He tried to bite down on his anxiety. "I'm sorry. But I can't find her… And the glass in the shed is all shattered… And there is blood! I was hoping she was over here." The words tumbled out and pushed him over the edge. *Something was seriously wrong.* He dialed 911.

"911, what is your emergency?" the switchboard operator said.

Jordan yelled, "My wife is missing, and the shed's glass window is shattered, and there is blood everywhere!" Jordan heard bangs and screams from across the street. He shoved his phone to Mr. Platte and ran towards the commotion.

Mr. Platte raised the phone to his ear and told the operator, "Something bad is happening. Better make it quick. We are at 2411 South James Road, but the screams are coming from 2414 South James Road. So, you better get here quick."

Jordan was across the road and up the gravel driveway beside Anita and Roger's house in seconds. Then he stopped dead in his tracks. A lanky young man with a blood-stained tee shirt rushed by him.

"Bailey?" Jordan asked.

The man looked at Jordan, jerked his head toward the garage, and kept going. Police sirens grew louder as Jordan watched the man move down the driveway toward the Platte's. He turned back toward the garage and saw Bailey in Anita's chokehold.

"Bailey!" Jordan asked.

From behind him, Jordan heard, "Freeze. Put your hands up!

Jordan did what he was told but kept his eyes on the scene in the garage. "I called 911. Anita is attacking my wife!" he yelled and pointed.

Two cops rushed up the driveway past Jordan, who kept his hands up. A third cop crept around the house, over the pecan stump to flank his colleagues on the side of the garage, and a fourth stopped next to Jordan, his gun drawn.

"You can put your hands down, sir, but you must leave the area. It isn't safe. Officer Page is down there, and he will take your statement." The officer pointed with his chin.

Jordan looked down at the street. "Like hell," he yelled.

The cop looked at Jordan. "A crazed husband in the crossfire won't help anyone. So, stay back and take cover. This is a dangerous situation here."

"If my wife dies, it won't matter." Jordan ran up the rest of the length of the driveway with Officer Do-Good on his heels. *Shoot me if you need to.* He was ten feet from the opening when he stopped. Three cops pointed guns at three people inside the garage: Bailey, Anita, and Roger.

Roger stood covered in dirt, dazed, while Anita still had Bailey in a chokehold. *This isn't good.* Jordan took five paces back, right into Officer Do-Good. The officer placed his hand on Jordan's shoulder and forced him to kneel.

"Don't let Anita kill my wife!" Jordan pleaded.

43: Bailey

4:20 p.m.

Bailey stared out the crack from her perch at the door. "Kurt, are you ready?" She looked over her shoulder.

Kurt was in the opposite corner with a rake and a small plastic bucket in one hand. Bailey paused on his so-called weapons. *It wasn't much. Defend yourself with a plastic bucket. Sure, that will work.* Her ambitious getaway plan would either be the silliest way to die or an act of pure brilliance.

She liked how Kurt was all on board with the idea. But simultaneously, it also scared the hell out of her. *What if I'm wrong?* Yet, it was the best plan she could think of at the moment. *Either way, we're fucked, so let's go for broke.*

"Here we go!" Bailey announced.

She banged on the door and screamed at the top of her lungs. Her throat quickly got dry, and she wished she had taken some of Kurt's water. But it didn't stop her. She continued until she could see Anita at the kitchen door. Bailey stepped back and waited as her eyes adjusted to the darkness. Kurt hid behind the tower of plastic tubs they had stacked earlier. Bailey hoped she was far enough back not to be seen.

A moment later, the door flew open.

Just as Kurt predicted, Anita was in front. The daylight shadowed Anita's face, but Bailey could see her eyes as they glowed red. Roger was two steps behind her.

"Bailey, where the fuck are you?" Anita screamed. She stepped inside, just on edge between light and dark, hands-on-hips.

"Right here, bitch!" Bailey screamed back.

While Bailey diverted their attention from the right side, Kurt stepped out from behind the tub tower and swung the rake at Roger, catching him in the stomach. As Roger bent over in pain, Kurt picked up a tub of granular fertilizer and dumped it over his head. Once the tub was empty, Kurt covered Roger's head with it and banged on the sides to disorientate Roger. On his way out of the garage, Kurt shoved Roger aside. Roger fell to his knees and fumbled to get the tub off his head.

Bailey stepped forward and swung at Anita's midsection with the shovel. Anita blocked the swing, grabbed the shovel's shaft, and pulled it out of Bailey's hands. *That didn't go well. That bitch is strong!*

Anita looked at the shovel like it was the first time she had ever held one. Then she raised it like a baseball bat and aimed. Bailey crouched down and yanked on the hose she had placed on the ground to encircle Anita's feet. With one quick move, the hose tightened, and Anita stumbled further into the darkness of the garage.

Bailey turned to head outside herself, but Roger grabbed her foot. She tripped and fell on her side. Roger flipped her onto her back and straddled her at the waist. Anita scrambled across the ground, pushed Roger off Bailey, and punched her in the stomach.

Blood dripped from the corners of Anita's mouth and nose. Anita wiped her nose with her hand and stared at the blood. "You did this to me. You're going to hell for this!" she screamed. "It's all your fault."

How? Her face didn't even hit the ground. "My fault?" Bailey asked as she struggled to get up.

Roger sat on his butt, knees bent close to his chin, hands over his ears. He rocked back and forth, "Make it stop, make it stop."

Anita paused and looked at him. "Roger, are you okay?"

Roger stared at Anita. "Why do you care now?"

Her voice was cool and had a sinister tone. "Roger. I have always cared about you." She wiped her nose again.

Bailey didn't like the mood swings she was witnessing from Anita. She didn't know what was going on between them, but she rammed the heel of her hand into Anita's nose. Bones broke under the flesh. Anita cried out in pain and fell off Bailey's stomach.

"Anita!" Roger crawled over and wrapped his arms around her.

Bailey scrambled to get up, but Roger extended a leg and tripped her again. It took Bailey two giant steps forward before she recovered her balance. Anita got to her feet, too, and charged Bailey from behind.

As she stood straight, she felt Anita's arm wrap around her neck in a chokehold. Bailey instinctively turned her head to get her chin hooked in the elbow's crook and avoid a crushed voice box. Anita was taller than Bailey and had to stand on her tiptoes so the grip wouldn't hurt. Bailey's legs, feet, and toes started to cramp. *Not the time for a charley horse.*

In the bright sunlight, Bailey saw the police with their guns drawn, though she seemed to be the only one who noticed. *Why aren't they doing anything? Shoot her already!*

"Roger, why are you just sitting there? Help me with this bitch!" Anita screamed at Roger, who looked lost.

Roger looks defeated. Bailey focused on Roger's expressions. She watched as sadness changed to anger.

"Roger!" Anita screamed again.

He didn't look at her when he responded. "It's over, Anita. Let her go. It's all over." Roger turned his head just enough to acknowledge the police's presence. "It's over."

Bailey noticed the remorseful tone in his voice. It almost sounded like he was sorry for their actions. *Are you fucking kidding me? Crazy ass neighbors made our lives hell, and one of them feels sorry?*

"No. It is not over until the person who did this to me pays!" Anita jerked her arm, and Bailey's feet left the ground. "She is going to pay!"

Bailey begged, "What did I do?"

Anita shook Bailey by the neck. "You fucking cut the pecan tree down! And then you cut the other one down! You made me sick!"

"What? How?" Bailey chirped. She tugged at Anita's arm and gasped out a response. "We cut down the tree? Do you mean the tree you and your crazy husband have wanted gone for the past ten years? And what other tree?"

Anita squeezed tighter. Through gritted teeth, she said, "The tree in the front hedge."

Bailey snapped back, "The alder?"

"Stop! Just stop!" Roger yelled from his perch and rocked back and forth again. "Just stop, Anita. Bailey didn't make you sick by cutting down the pecan tree."

"Roger.... The bats came from that tree!"

Why the hell is she talking about bats? The bats still live behind their shutters.

"No. You were sick before the tree came down, remember?" Roger paused, and his expression changed from anger to defeat. "All I ever wanted to do was to live on my own. I am tired of living with my sister!"

Wait? What? They're siblings?

"I love you, Roger. You know that. I was doing all of this for you, my little brother. For us. So, we could get away from this place." Anita cried.

His expression changed back to anger. "Oh really? Well, how about if I told you I was the one who got you sick? I poisoned you!"

Bailey heard a little whimper from Anita and felt hot breath on her neck as Anita huffed.

Roger stood and pointed a finger at Anita. "For the past year, I have been sprinkling that damn doll Papa brought home from Germany with dried-up bat crap!"

Eww. Bailey felt Anita's grip relax. *This may be my chance.*

"What are you talking about?" Anita asked. Her voice had changed from furious to calm.

Too calm, Bailey noted.

Roger continued. "I collected it on my nightly walks."

Ah, that would explain the black tracksuit and the lurking around in the dark.

"I hoped you would die like Mama after only a couple of weeks, but here we are." He waved his arm in a large arc.

"I don't understand."

"Either the virus mutated, or with all your research, you created an antibody without knowing it." Roger avoided Anita's gaze. Instead, he focused on the gravel as he shifted from side to side.

"You poisoned me?"

"Anita, I didn't mean to… I'm sorry. After you got the results back, I regretted what I had done. Then, I convinced myself that because you were sick, it would prompt you to solve the problem. You would have the cure, and then you could be the hero. Then you could save your own life and anyone else who contracted the disease."

"You poisoned me?"

Everything became still momentarily, like someone had pressed *pause* on a movie scene. Roger stopped kicking the gravel, and the cops outside stood like statues with guns ready. Bailey held her breath. *This is the critical moment.*

Distracted by Roger's confession, Anita released Bailey and charged Roger. She reached for her brother and grabbed him by the neck. Anita, taller than Roger, lifted him off the ground and shook him like a dog does with a stuffed toy.

Bailey fell to her knees and rolled left towards the garage door opening. She felt a hand on her arm and saw a cop pull her up and past him as she stumbled out of the garage. Ahead, Jordan had his arms out, his face red and wet with tears. She fell into his arms and buried her head in his chest.

"Put your hands up! Hands up!" The police screamed, then three gunshots rang out.

44: Channel 8 News

4:45 p.m.

Deep inside the Platte's house, the little black-and-white TV in the kitchen broadcast breaking news to an empty room.

"Happening now!" the voice from a newscaster belted out. "Robbins Meadow, a quiet and close-knit neighborhood south of downtown Charlotte, has been rocked by violence. We have Bonnie Wagner on the scene. Bonnie, can you give us any details on this breaking news?"

A woman in her thirties with dark brown hair nodded to the camera before she spoke. "Thanks, Dan. We are at the corner of South James Road and Route 4, just inside the neighborhood of Robbins Meadow." She turned and pointed to Anita and Roger's house as the camera operator panned out to give a wide-angle view.

She then turned back to the camera. "As you can see, this is an active crime scene. So far, Charlotte Police haven't issued a shelter-in-place order, though we are being held back for our safety." She looked down at her notepad. "We arrived at this volatile scene just before 4 p.m. As we were setting up, we heard gunshots."

She stepped out of camera view but continued to speak. The camera operator panned out and focused on the house across the street. "Three police vehicles are blocking a clear view of what is happening. It appears that at least two or three people outside that garage may be victims. But we don't know if the gunshots hit them. I want to repeat there is no 'shelter-in-place' order. The scene is now secure."

"At this time, the police haven't released a statement, but rest assured, we will update you with more details as they come. This is Bonnie Wanger, reporting for Channel Eight News from Charlotte. Back to you in the studio, Dan."

"Bonnie, thank you for your report. I am glad to know you are safe." Dan said.

5:00 p.m.

Bonnie now stood in front of a stately two-story brick colonial. In the video's corner, yellow crime scene tape fluttered. She waited for the sign she was live again, then spoke, "The activity here at the corner of South James Road and Route 4 has settled, as it appears the police have moved into investigation mode. Here is the updated information for our viewers."

Bonnie looked down at her notepad before she continued. "I can confirm two people are dead, identified as Anita and Roger Belo, the owners of the residence at 2414 South James Road. In addition, two people are being treated for injuries, but it is unclear if those injuries are life-threatening. Both victims have been taken to County General for treatment."

"We learned the two injured victims, a male in his early 20s and a female in her 40s, were being held against their will in the Belo's garage. The circumstances surrounding their kidnapping remain unclear, but we know the female lives at 2412 South James Road, next door to the deceased."

She pointed to the house behind her. "We've been asked not to disclose their identities at this time. Neighbors describe a history of turmoil between the two couples over the last few months. It has been reported that tensions began with the cutting down of a pecan tree between the two properties. The only thing left is a stump." Bonnie moved out of the camera shot and let the operator focus on the massive trunk. "Though we have no details as to what transpired, today marks a violent end to that confrontation."

6:30 p.m.

"We are learning more in our continuing coverage of the Robbins Meadow shooting. Starting in September, seven Fairview University students became ill, and two died after contracting a mystery illness, now identified as Marburg Hemorrhagic Fever, commonly known as Bat Crap Fever. A cure was being researched at the University by Professor Anita Belo. Colleagues of Belo described her as a brilliant researcher. For the last ten years, she has been researching to find a cure for the virus. It's now known that, while working on the cure, Belo contracted the same disease. New evidence reveals that once she was self-diagnosed with the deadly disease, she deliberately exposed students to the virus to accelerate her research for a cure, knowing it was only a matter of time before she would succumb to the deadly disease herself. Historically, the virus's progression spans only three weeks before ending in death. However, it is unclear why Belo's case lasted beyond the three weeks."

"Yesterday, in a news conference, a spokesperson for the university officially denounced all research Belo performed during her time at the school."

"In related news, a research team from Neu Leben Laboratories in Marburg, Germany, announced earlier today that they have successfully stabilized a vaccine for the Marburg Hemorrhagic Fever, the same virus Belo was working to cure."

Acknowledgments

Which came first, the chicken or the egg? It has always been a debate. It is the same for writing this book. So, in no particular order, I want to thank the following people:

I want to thank my critique partners, Anne F., Sherry C., and Susan A., who spent as much time with Bat Crap Crazy as I have. Your comments, questions, and suggestions made this book much better than the rough draft I started eleven years ago.

To my beta readers, Chris R., Katy V., Marcus H., and Mike K. were the first to read and edit the complete book. Again, your comments, questions, and suggestions made this book much more appealing.

To my professional proofreader, Dave P., who took one last look at the book and made sure I had all my commas and periods in place.

To all the people in the supportive community of Shut Up & Write's weekday sessions, like so many in this group, you have been part of the process.

I want to thank all my supportive family and friends who helped me throughout the journey.

Bonnie M., a career counselor I met with back in the day who, told me I was intelligent.

To the ones who are no longer with me on earth but still greatly influence me every day.

And always and forever, I want to thank Marcus. I love you very much and appreciate the time and space you have given me to see this project through to the end. Also, I thank Kie and the late Scarpa for being the best supervisors a writer could hope to have.

CJ Hanlon marvels in disbelief at the world around her every day. It's why she writes. It helps her understand or at least come to terms with what she experiences.

Hanlon is fascinated by life's choices and their consequences. Her conclusions form the backbone of her writing in the genres of mystery/thriller, satire, and nonfiction self-development. She weaves her curiosity, dark humor, and independent nature into each facet.

CJ Hanlon lives in Colorado with her husband and furry work supervisor, Kie, a wheaten terrier. When she isn't writing, she enjoys other creative outlets like cooking, baking, and photography. She is also always on the lookout for good food and drink in quiet, cozy public places.

Connect with her on Facebook and Instagram @cjhanlonwrites or visit her website at www.cjhanlonwrites.com.

www.ingramcontent.com/pod-product-compliance
Lightning Source LLC
LaVergne TN
LVHW090604110826
845146LV00001B/253

9798990526907